STORYSLAVE

BRIAN BOWYER

UNCOMFORTABLY DARK HORROR

Book Cover by Christy Aldridge

First edition 2025

Edited & formatted by 360 Editing (a division of Uncomfortably Dark Horror).

Editor: Candace Nola

Published by Uncomfortably Dark Horror. Pittsburgh, PA 15202

"Bringing you the best in horror, one Uncomfortably Dark page at a time."

Follow us on all social media, join our Patreon, and check out our website to order signed copies of all our books!

CONTENTS

ALSO BY BRIAN BOWYER

PRAISE FOR BRIAN BOWYER

"Brian Bowyer is a master of extreme horror. You've been warned!" —Ross Jeffery, Bram Stoker Award-nominated author of *Tome, Beautiful Atrocities,* and *The Devil's Pocketbook.*

"Brian Bowyer is one of the greatest writers of our generation. Years from now, if there's any justice, his work will be studied." —Judith Sonnet, author of *Summer Never Ends* and *No One Rides for Free.*

PART ONE: SCARLETT

CHAPTER 1

MYLA DIDN'T WANT TO meet Archibald. After the year she had just endured, Myla had no interest in meeting anyone. First, her daughter got bone cancer: diagnosis at five; dead and gone by the time she was six years old. Then her husband left her for her sister.

"And what the hell kind of a name is Archibald, anyway?" Myla said.

"It's unusual," Katelyn admitted. "But it fits him. He's an unusual man."

Katelyn and Myla sold Manhattan real estate. They were in their late twenties. They shared an office on West 42nd Street.

"Archibald," Myla said. "I wouldn't name a dog Archibald."

"He's very attractive," Katelyn said.

"It's a terrible name." Myla stared at her computer screen, looking at SoHo prices. She wore a designer suit and expensive shoes. "It's like the name of a villain in a movie."

"This isn't a movie," Katelyn said. "This is your life, and you need to start living it again."

It was almost five p.m. on a Thursday. Their office was on the twenty-fourth floor. Beyond the bay window facing south, two rivers shimmered in the sunlight: the East and the Hudson.

"How do you know this Archibald?" Myla said.

Katelyn shrugged. "I've known him for a while, but I don't remember where I met him. He's the curator of an art gallery in Brooklyn."

Myla shot her a look. "A curator?"

"Yes, but don't let the title fool you. Archibald's filthy rich. He's thinking about opening his own gallery here in Manhattan."

Though neither had yet turned thirty, Katelyn and Myla were worth about five million dollars each.

"How did he acquire his fortune?" Myla said.

"I don't know. He's very secretive."

"How old is he?"

"I'm not sure. I think he's older than us, but I'm not positive. He seems older, anyway. But he still looks young. He's very attractive."

"Yes, you told me that already. What's his last name?"

"Look," Katelyn said. "I don't know much about him. All I know is that he's rich, he's good-looking, he's thinking about opening an art gallery in Manhattan, and that he's ready to meet a woman."

"Ready to meet a woman?"

"Yes. That's how he put it. Those were his exact words. He told me that he was ready to meet a woman."

"When did he tell you this?"

"Last night. At a bar."

"Which bar?"

"JoJo's Lantern."

"JoJo's Lantern? Over on Bleecker Street?"

"Yes."

"Isn't that a restaurant, too?"

"Yes."

"I heard they have good food."

"They do. Anyway, Archibald told me that he was ready to meet a woman, and then I told him about you."

"Why me?" Myla said. "Why did you tell him about me?"

"Because it's time you moved on from the past," Katelyn said. "Also, Archibald mentioned that he's leery of meeting women who would only want to be with him because of his money. When I told him that you were independently wealthy, he breathed a sigh of relief."

"What else did you tell him about me?"

"Not much. I told him you were divorced. I told him you lost a daughter to cancer about a year ago. And I told him about how much you love to draw, of course. About your interest in art. He was very happy to hear about that. I showed him a photo of you. Needless to say, he thinks you're beautiful."

"Do you have any pictures of him?"

Katelyn shook her head. "No. I'm not connected with Archibald through any social media. I *do* have his phone number, though. Do you want it?"

Myla shrugged. "Sure. Why not? I suppose it couldn't hurt to meet him."

CHAPTER 2

SHE CALLED HIM. THEY spoke briefly and exchanged a few text messages. They agreed to meet at JoJo's Lantern on Saturday night.

Myla drove. Archibald was waiting at a table by a window when she arrived. The table had a candle on it. The window provided a view of traffic on East Fourth Street.

"Hello, Archibald." She held a hand out. "I'm Myla."

Archibald stood up. He smiled, and she noticed that he had nice teeth. He was tall, too. He looked the same as he appeared in the photo he had sent to her phone: dark brown eyes; a full head of thick brown hair; a lean face with sharp, angular features. He was forty years old but didn't look a day over thirty.

He shook her hand. "Nice to meet you."

They sat down.

"Steak," Archibald said, when the waitress came for their order. "Medium rare. Baked potato. Diet soda."

"Grilled chicken," Myla said. "Side salad. French dressing. Ginger ale."

They ate in silence for a while, and then Archibald said, "Katelyn told me you like to draw."

Myla nodded. "That's true."

"Are you any good?"

She took a pen from her purse, quickly sketched his face on a napkin, and slid it across the table.

His dark eyes lit up as soon as he saw it, and he smiled. "Oh my. This is spectacular! It looks just like me." He took a photo of the portrait with his phone. Then he folded the napkin carefully and put it in his pocket. "I'll keep it forever."

"Katelyn told me you're a curator," Myla said.

He nodded.

"In Brooklyn?"

"Yes."

"What gallery?"

"Paracosmos. Ever heard of it?"

"No, but I love that name."

"So do I."

"Is that even a word?"

He cocked his head. "I'm not sure. I know *paracosm* is a word. Do you know what a paracosm is?"

Myla took a sip of ginger ale. "Yes. I remember the term from an old psychology course. A paracosm is a highly detailed imaginary world, usually created by a child."

Archibald sipped his diet soda. "Yes. Paracosms often have their own geographies, histories, languages . . . all kinds of fascinating stuff."

"So I guess," Myla said, "that a paracosmos would be a universe consisting of paracosms created by children."

Archibald smiled. "Or artists." Then his smile quickly disappeared. "And speaking of children: Katelyn told me about your daughter. I'm sorry for your loss."

"Thanks." Myla glanced out the window. Pedestrians and vehicles were streaming in both directions on East Fourth Street.

"Cancer, was it?"

"Yes. Bone cancer."

"How old was she?"

"Six. Her name was Miriam, by the way. Miriam was six years old when she died."

"Who knows?" Archibald sipped his soda. "Perhaps Miriam's in a paracosm of her own, right now, as we speak."

Myla shrugged. "It's a comforting thought. But a paracosm, by definition, is imaginary."

They ate in silence briefly. Then Archibald said, "Katelyn told me you've recently divorced."

Myla looked up from her plate. "I wouldn't call it recent. Miriam's been dead for a year, and Nick left me right after she died."

"A lot of marriages," Archibald said, "do not survive the loss of a child."

Myla cocked her head. "That wasn't it at all."

"It wasn't?"

"No. Didn't Katelyn tell you?"

"She told me you were divorced. She didn't go into detail."

"Nick left me for my sister. Marlow."

"Oh my," Archibald said. "I had no idea. How awful."

"Yes," Myla said. "I was devastated. Marlow's only a year older than me. She had always been my best friend, you know? My rock. My mainstay. I loved her as much as I loved my daughter and my husband. And here's what's *really* fucked up. Right after Miriam died, Nick and Marlow revealed to me that not only were they in love, but that they had been having an affair behind my back since even before Miriam was diagnosed with bone cancer. The two of them got married not long after my divorce from Nick was finalized. So yeah, it's been a rough year for me. In the past twelve months, I've lost my daughter, my husband, and my sister—who was also my lifelong best friend." Myla sipped her ginger ale. "Definitely a difficult year."

Archibald shook his head. "I don't even know what to say about that."

"So don't say anything. Tell me about yourself."

He shook his head again. "No. Tell me about your art."

"My art?"

"Yes."

"What about it?"

He took a sip of soda. "Well, you're obviously very good at drawing. Do you possess similar skills with a paintbrush?"

"I don't know," she admitted. "I've yet to paint anything, in fact."

"And why is that?"

"Because I'm waiting for a story to tell."

"Is that right?"

"Yes. Some whisper, and others scream, but all works of art must say something. And I definitely want my first painting to say something. I'm waiting for a story to tell."

"There's a painting," Archibald said, "with quite a story at Paracosmos that would probably interest you."

"Oh really?"

"Yes. Supposedly, the painting is haunted."

"Haunted?"

"Yes. Do you believe in ghosts?"

"Absolutely." Myla took a drink of ginger ale. "I grew up in a haunted house, so I definitely know a thing or two about ghosts."

"Personally," Archibald said, "I have no experience with ghosts. And the painting has never communicated with me. Apparently, it doesn't speak to just anyone. But I *can* tell you that the painting has spooked so many customers in the brief time we've had it that we've deemed it inappropriate for public viewing."

"Really?"

"Yes. It's no longer on display. We keep it in a back room of the gallery."

"Well, you've certainly piqued my interest," Myla said. "Tell me more."

"It's a painting by Steven Alenzo. Ever heard of him?"

Myla's eyes widened. "Steven Alenzo? Isn't he the artist who tortured and killed all those people?"

"Yes. Allegedly."

"Did they ever find him?"

Archibald—finished with his meal—put his fork down and pushed his plate to the edge of the table for the waitress. "No. He managed to avoid apprehension. He fled before he was ever arrested. So now he's just been a fugitive from justice for a decade."

Myla, too, pushed her plate to the edge of the table. "Wow. Ten years is a long time to be on the run from the law."

He nodded. "Yes, it is."

She finished her ginger ale. "So how did you end up with this supposedly haunted painting of his, anyway?"

"A young woman from Brooklyn brought it to us at Paracosmos. She never told us her name, how she acquired the painting, or anything else of that nature. She said she was hearing voices in her head, and claimed that the painting was talking to her. She also said the painting was causing her to experience intense headaches, and she just wanted to get rid of it. I don't even know if she knew that the artist is wanted for murder, even though Steven Alenzo's signature is right there on the bottom of the canvas. She passed the painting along to us at no cost whatsoever, and then we never saw the woman again."

"Interesting. Does the painting have a title?"

"Yes." Archibald finished his diet soda. "*Blood Moon Rising.* Alenzo put the title on the back of the painting."

Myla leaned forward. "I want to see it."

"Tonight?"

"Yes."

"Well, the gallery's closed, but of course I have a key. You feel like going to Brooklyn?"

"Yes."

"You want to ride with me?"

Myla shook her head. "No. I'll follow you in my car."

"Very well."

Archibald summoned the waitress, and she brought their bill. He paid for their dinner with a credit card at the service desk.

Then Myla followed him to Paracosmos in Brooklyn. It took them about an hour to get there. The gallery was in a one-story brick building. They parked in front of the building and went inside.

He led her to a hallway in the back. She followed him down the hallway to a door marked STORAGE. He took a ring of keys from his pocket, found the correct one, and unlocked the door. Then he opened the door and turned on a light.

They stepped into a room cluttered with boxes and mounted canvases covered by drop cloths. He led her to one of the canvases leaning against a wall and removed its cloth.

"*Blood Moon Rising,*" Archibald said. "By Steven Alenzo."

"Oh wow," Myla said. "That is a stunning piece of work."

The background was a starry sky, and superimposed over it was the transparent face of a beautiful young girl. She appeared to be about five or six years old. She had long red hair and bright green eyes. Her eyes were turned upward, toward a wash of light that rained down upon her from beyond the top of the canvas. The yellow light looked warm and inviting, but the expression on the little girl's face and in her eyes conveyed absolute sorrow. In the foreground, as the focus of the painting, a red moon rose over an ocean. Alenzo's signature was in the bottom-left corner of the canvas. The artist had signed his name in the same shade of red as the blood moon rising over the ocean—which was a darker red than the hair of the little girl whose sad, transparent face was superimposed over the stars in the background.

"That's the saddest little girl I've ever seen," Myla said. "She looks to be about the same age that Miriam was when she died."

"Your daughter was six, right?"

Myla nodded. "Yes. And this painting is definitely haunted. The little girl is whispering in my head as we speak."

"What's she saying?"

"I don't know. I can't make her words out. Just murmurs and faint susurrations. And a melody! Yes! Now she's humming a soft melody, like a lullaby. You can't hear that?"

"No. Like I said: the painting has never communicated to me, but it spooked so many customers that we deemed it inappropriate for public viewing. That is why we keep it back here in storage."

"I wonder who this little girl is," Myla said. "One of his victims?"

Archibald nodded. "Evidently. It's an acrylic painting, of course, but there's also two types of human blood mixed in with the red acrylic."

"Human blood?" She took a step back from the canvas and turned to face him. "How do you know?"

"Before we yanked it from public view, several customers claimed that the little girl in the painting told them that the artist used her blood to paint the moon."

"I still can't make out what she's saying." Myla cocked her head. "She's still whispering, though. So anyway, what did you do? Have someone pull samples from the canvas for testing?"

"Yes. Two different blood types came back. One was found in the paint used for the moon. The other was found in the paint used for the signature."

She put a hand on her hip. "Let me guess: Steven Alenzo's blood type matches the signature?"

"Correct. Which means, of course, that unless all those customers were lying, the blood in the paint used for the moon came from the little girl's body."

She took a step closer to the canvas. "How much do you want for this?"

"You can just have it," Archibald said. "The painting doesn't speak to me, but lately I've been getting terrible headaches."

"Thank you. You're very generous. And speaking of headaches, I need to get home and take my medication. I'll call you sometime."

He nodded. "Please do. It was nice to meet you."

"Likewise."

She took *Blood Moon Rising* back to her apartment in Manhattan.

CHAPTER 3

MYLA'S PHONE RANG AND woke her from a nightmare about Steven Alenzo. In her dream, the fugitive artist had been cutting her flesh with a straight razor and a carving knife. Also in her dream, he had looked about the same as the last time she had seen him on the news, probably ten years ago. For once, she was glad she had forgotten to turn down her cellphone's ringtone volume before falling asleep.

Her phone was on the nightstand by her bed. She picked it up and cringed when she saw who was calling her. She thought about not answering, but decided to accept the call. She took a deep breath and then pressed the TALK button. "Hello?"

"Hi, Myla! I hope I didn't wake you." Her sister was trying to make her voice sound cheerful.

"Don't worry about it. But I *do* have a headache, so let's keep this brief."

"Ah. Still the resentment, I see. Even after all this time. I'm still your sister, Myla. You need to get over it."

I will never get over what you did to me, Myla thought. *I will never get over what both of you did to me.*

"What do you want, Marlow?"

"Nick left a couple of photo albums in the attic at your house. Old photographs from his side of the family. He'd like to get them back."

"Okay. I'll look for them later. When I feel better. If I find them, I'll send them to you."

"We're not doing anything today. I can come over by myself and help you look for them. Would that be okay?"

The last thing Myla wanted was to see Marlow. A year had passed since she and Nick revealed their affair, but that was a wound that would always be raw. "No. Listen, I already told you that I don't feel good. I have to go."

"But—"

Myla stopped the call and tossed her phone onto Nick's old side of the bed. Her head wasn't hurting. That had been a lie. It had also been a lie when she told Archibald that her head was hurting last night. But the little girl's voice in her head was pretty much ceaseless. And some of her words were starting to come through clearly now, too. It was like there were no other voices in the world anymore. There was only the little girl's voice, speaking to her. Ever since last night, Myla's entire existence seemed to be quickly becoming only the little girl's voice in her mind. *Blood Moon Rising* was hanging on the wall above her headboard, but she didn't need to be looking at the painting to hear the little girl's voice.

Myla closed her eyes. She didn't think she would go back to sleep, but she did. She dreamed about Steven Alenzo making her bleed.

CHAPTER 4

THE NEXT DAY, WHILE leaving for work on Monday morning, Myla's head started hurting as soon as she left her apartment. By the time she arrived at the office, her pain was excruciating.

"How did it go with Archibald?" Katelyn said.

Myla shrugged. "Not bad, I suppose. But he's definitely not my type."

Katelyn gave her a look of concern. "Are you okay? My god, Myla, you look terrible."

Myla pressed a hand to her forehead. "Bad migraine. I think I should go back home. Actually, I think I should just take some time off work for a while."

Katelyn nodded. "I agree. I've been telling you that for a year now. Take a few weeks and put yourself back together. Hell, take a few *months*, if you need to. It's not like you can't afford it."

"I'll call you soon," Myla said.

She left. By the time she got back to her apartment, the headache had gone away completely.

CHAPTER 5

ONE WEEK LATER. FOUR a.m. Awake on her sofa.

The little girl was talking, and Myla's head wasn't hurting at all. She had moved the painting from her bedroom into the living room and it was now hanging on the wall above her television. The TV was on, but she wasn't watching it. The volume was turned all the way down. She had learned fairly quickly that there was a direct correlation between the pain in her head and her proximity to *Blood Moon Rising.* As long as she stayed close to the painting, her head remained free of pain. If she didn't stay close to the painting, the pain returned and became increasingly worse the farther she withdrew.

She was almost asleep when the little girl said something that caused Myla's eyelids to snap open. "Sorry," Myla said. "I was almost asleep. Could you repeat that, please?"

I said the bad man has another little girl.

"Who? Steven Alenzo?"

Yes. The bad man. The man who used my blood to paint the moon. He has another little girl now, and he's taking her to the same place he took me.

"How do you know this?"

Because sometimes I can see out of the bad man's eyes. Sometimes I can see what the bad man sees. He's taking her to the place where the big moose lives.

"The big moose?"

Yes. The big moose lives on the side of the road.

"Does the big moose live in New York?"

I don't know. It was really far away in a car. It's a place called Upstate. That's what the bad man kept telling me. He kept saying that he was taking me to a place called Upstate.

Upstate, Myla knew, was basically what most people called the entire state of New York, north of New York City. The girl in the painting could have been (unknowingly) referring to Albany, Buffalo, Rochester, Syracuse, or any one of a thousand other places, but as soon as she had mentioned a big moose that lives on the side of a road, Myla had a suspicion that she knew exactly where the little girl was talking about.

As a child growing up in Manhattan, Myla's parents had often driven her through a lot of rural areas in the state of New York's northern regions during vacations and weekend getaways, and an image that remained lodged in her memory even after all these years was the statue of a giant moose on the side of a road up in the Catskill Mountains, about a hundred miles north of New York City. The statue had served as a signpost for a large campgrounds area called Moose Mountain Cabins. Myla's parents had rented cabins there a few times during her childhood, and she had contemplated going back there by herself and renting a cabin sometime now that she was an adult.

"Moose Mountain Cabins," Myla said. "Is that where the bad man took you?"

Yes. He took me to a cabin where the moose lives.

"And now he's taking another girl to a cabin where the moose lives?"

Yes. He wants to use her blood to make another painting. And then he wants to kill her, just like he killed me.

CHAPTER 6

WHILE MYLA SLEPT, SHE struggled through a series of dreams consisting of seemingly disassociated images that melded into one another with no logical narrative flow whatsoever.

Wind-whipped rain. Groves of leafless trees. Lightning and thunder.

Her lost daughter, Miriam, lying with sallow skin and hollow cheeks against hospital sheets, dying of bone cancer.

Her sister and her ex-husband (her sister's husband, now) making love atop a grand piano in a ballroom, while a corpse conducted an orchestra of skeletons playing a symphony on a stage.

Frequently she was a passenger in a car driven by Steven Alenzo, and he referred to her as Scarlett, as if that were her name. At other times, he was not simply a part of the dream, but was instead the viewpoint through which the dream was observed, as if Myla were actually looking out at the world through Steven Alenzo's eyes—and that was how she learned that Scarlett was the name of the little girl whose face was in the painting. The name of the little girl whose blood he had used to paint the moon in *Blood Moon Rising* was Scarlett.

CHAPTER 7

MYLA WOKE UP AND decided that she needed to kill Steven Alenzo. She didn't know if she had come to that decision on her own, or if Scarlett had helped her reach it in her sleep. Either way, it was something that needed to be done. Maybe then Scarlett's soul would be released from *Blood Moon Rising*, and perhaps Myla would then be free of the control the painting was holding her under.

But first she had to find him, which was something the authorities had been unable to do for the past ten years. The authorities, however, didn't know where to look for him.

Myla did.

SHE NEEDED TO LEAVE the apartment to make a few purchases. Because she couldn't get too far away from the painting without being clobbered by headaches, Myla took it off her wall and put it in the trunk of her car. Then she drove to a sporting-goods store on Fifth Avenue.

Leaving *Blood Moon Rising* in the trunk, she went inside. She was able to do her shopping without experiencing any head pain.

CHAPTER 8

IS THAT A GUN?

Myla was sitting on her sofa in the living room, holding a crossbow. The rest of her purchases from the sporting-goods store were spread out on the coffee table. The painting was once again hanging on the wall above the television. Scarlett's eyes in *Blood Moon Rising* were, as always, looking up at the light shining down upon her face from beyond the top of the canvas, but the little girl could evidently still see her nevertheless.

"No," Myla said. "I have a gun, but it's in my bedroom. This is a crossbow."

What's a crossbow?

"A weapon that shoots arrows."

Like what Cupid uses?

Myla smiled. "Something like that."

Do you know how to shoot it?

"Oh yes. I used to win trophies for archery when I was a little girl."

What's archery?

"Shooting arrows with a bow, basically. Before that, I took ballet lessons at Miss Llewellyn's, on the Upper West Side."

I know what ballet is. I like ballet.

"Me too. Anyway, Miss Llewellyn used to watch my body carefully, to see if I had a future in ballet. Rumor had it that Miss Llewellyn was a fortune teller. Supposedly, she had gypsy blood running through her veins. People said that she could read a girl's destiny in the way she moved her limbs and her body. One day, she tapped me on the shoulder and told me that I was not a dancer. She told me that I was an archer, instead. And that was all it took for me. I went straight home and told my parents that I wanted to switch from ballet to archery."

How old were you?

"Nine, I think. Maybe ten. Something like that."

Oh.

"So how old were you, Scarlett? How old were you when you died?"

Six.

"I had a daughter. Her name was Miriam. She was six years old when she died."

Did a bad man kill her, too?

"No. Bone cancer killed Miriam."

What's bone cancer?

"A terrible illness."

Illness?

"A disease."

What's a disease?

"A really bad sickness."

Oh. So Miriam got sick, and then she died?

"Yes."

That's sad.

Myla set the crossbow down on the coffee table amongst her other purchases: binoculars; camouflage clothes; plenty of extra twenty-inch broadhead arrows; a hunting knife; a handheld directional compass with a lanyard to wear around her neck. "If I take you to where the moose lives, will you be able to help me find Steven Alenzo?"

Yes. If you get me close to the bad man, I can help you find him.

Myla nodded. "Okay then. Looks like you and I are headed to the Catskill Mountains."

Yay! If you can kill the bad man, maybe I can finally leave this stupid moon!

"That's the plan."

And maybe we can save the little girl, too!

"I suppose we'll see."

Myla packed her stuff into an extra-long duffel bag. Then she put *Blood Moon Rising* in the trunk of her car and hit the road.

CHAPTER 9

"Is that it?" Myla said, slowing the car as she approached the statue that served as a signpost for Moose Mountain Cabins. She had taken the painting from the trunk and put it on the seat behind her a few miles back.

Yes! That's it! That's the big moose that lives on the side of the road!

There were a few lay-bys on the road past the signpost. Myla parked in one of those and turned off the engine. She was dressed in the camouflage clothes and wearing gloves. Her duffel bag was on the passenger's seat beside her.

She had grabbed her gun before leaving the apartment. She picked it up off the floorboard beneath the driver's seat and looked at it.

The gun—a Glock 26 9mm—was loaded with ten rounds in the clip and one in the chamber. It was a small, easy-to-conceal gun that packed a powerful punch. She had paid cash for it in the back room of a pawn shop not long after Nick left her. Unless she got caught holding it, the gun could not be traced back to her. According to the man who had sold it to her, the gun wasn't registered to anyone.

Her camouflage pants had deep side pockets. She put the gun in the pocket on her right side with plenty of room to spare.

You have to hurry! You have to kill the bad man before he kills the little girl!

"Do you know which cabin he's in?"

He's not in the cabin right now! He's walking around in the woods! He's going to use her blood to make a painting when he gets back to the cabin!

Myla opened her duffel bag. A strap was attached to the binoculars. She put the strap around her neck. She also put the lanyard attached to the compass around her neck. She put the hunting knife and a few spare arrows in her pocket on the left side of her camouflage pants. Then she grabbed the crossbow and got out of the car.

The day was young. The sky was gray. The temperature was mild. Woods of the Catskill Mountains lined both sides of the road. There were no cars going by in either direction.

Holding the crossbow in her right hand, Myla opened the rear door on the driver's side and grabbed *Blood Moon Rising* with her left. She took the painting out of the car and used a knee to close the door. It was a fairly large canvas, measuring two feet by three, but she could nevertheless carry it under her left arm with ease. "Which way?"

Turn around.

Myla did. She looked down at her compass. It was pointing north. "This way?"

Yes. There's water that way. His cabin is farther than the water.

Myla headed north through the woods. The part through which she walked was not very dense. Soon she came to a dirt road that went east and west with nice-looking rental cabins lined up on the other side of it.

The bad man went back inside his cabin.

"Which one is it? Is it one of these?"

No. His cabin is in the woods, past the water. There's a path behind these cabins that he uses.

"So just keep straight?"

Yes.

Myla crossed the road. Then she cut through the front yard of one of the rental cabins and went around back. There were more woods behind the cabins, and these woods, too, were not very thick. She walked until she came to a narrow trail that—according to the compass—continued to the north. "Is this the path?"

Yes. The bad man just came out of his cabin again.

"He did?"

Yes. Now he's walking back toward the water. He goes to the water to drink it and to take a bath.

Myla headed north up the path. The fact that Alenzo's cabin had no running water undoubtedly meant that his was not a rental. She didn't know how many privately owned cabins there were in the Catskill Mountains. Probably hundreds. Possibly thousands. She just hoped that Scarlett would be able to lead her to the right one.

She walked until she came to a shallow stream that flowed west to east. "Is this the water you were talking about?"

Yes.

"And his cabin's on the other side?"

Yes.

Myla crossed the stream. "Now what? Do I just keep straight?"

No.

She looked to the right. "This way?"

No.

She looked to the left. "That way?"

Yes.

Myla headed west along the stream.

There he is.

"Where? I don't see anything."

He's right up there.

Myla raised the binoculars. In the distance, straight ahead, a skinny bald man was kneeling at the water's edge with his hands down in the water.

She closed the gap between them, then crouched down in some weeds beside the path and zoomed in with the binoculars. She didn't know if he had lost his hair or had simply shaved his head, but she was definitely looking at Steven Alenzo's face. He pulled his hands from the water, and she saw that he had been cleaning a couple of paintbrushes. Then he stood and began walking north—presumably back to his cabin.

Myla lowered the binoculars and followed him. She kept to the trees and the weeds beside the path as she walked, with the painting beneath her left arm and the crossbow in her right hand. She only walked as quickly as he did. She intentionally refrained from closing the distance between them because she didn't want to alert him to her presence. Apparently, he never heard the sound of her footsteps. Not once did he turn around to see if there was anyone walking behind him.

She trailed him for about a mile, and then he took a left off the path and headed west through the woods. Myla followed.

It wasn't long before he reached a small cabin surrounded by maple trees. The cabin looked very old and had a chimney. Alenzo climbed three steps to the front porch.

Myla set the painting on the ground and leaned it against her leg. She cocked the crossbow and lifted it to her shoulder. She curled her finger around the trigger and targeted the center of his back. Then she waited for Alenzo to open the door.

He did.

"Your walking days are over," Myla whispered. Then she squeezed the trigger.

He dropped quickly. Myla set the crossbow down and picked up the painting. Then she grabbed the gun from her pocket and ran toward the cabin. She expected him to start screaming, but he never did.

He crawled inside the cabin, but she was already there before he could close the door. He was sitting on the floor, looking up at her. She had missed his spinal cord. The arrow was lodged in his body. The front half was sticking out of his abdomen. Blood dripped from the edges of the broadhead tip.

We're too late.

Scarlett was right, of course. They were definitely too late to save the girl.

Standing in the doorway, aiming her gun at Alenzo's face, Myla had already swept her gaze around the one-room cabin's interior. Curtains covered the two windows, but sunlight through the doorway provided plenty of illumination.

In the back of the room, near the left corner, the girl's decapitated corpse was hanging upside down from a rafter in the ceiling. She had not been dead for long. Blood was still draining from her corpse into an old clawfoot tub. Her severed head lay on the floor between the tub and a blank canvas that was mounted on an easel.

"*Blood Moon Rising,*" Steven Alenzo said. Still on the floor, he was looking up at the painting Myla held in the hand not aiming the gun at his forehead. "One of my old favorites. Where did you get it?"

Kill him! Please! Kill the bad man now!

"Brooklyn," Myla said. Then she pulled the trigger, killing him instantly. Also instantly, she stopped hearing Scarlett's voice inside her mind for the first time since setting her eyes on *Blood Moon Rising* in Paracosmos.

She tossed the painting down atop Alenzo's lifeless body. Then she swept her gaze around the room again.

The fugitive artist had powered the cabin with a generator. The generator used gasoline to produce electricity. She saw a plastic container of gasoline beside the generator and found a box of matches on the nightstand by his bed.

She doused *Blood Moon Rising* and Steven Alenzo's corpse with gasoline. Then she splashed gasoline throughout the interior of the cabin.

She stopped in front of the blank canvas mounted on the easel, ignoring the little girl's severed head on the floor. She had an easel set up at home in her living room, but she had yet to mount a canvas on it. She wanted her first painting to say something. She was waiting for a story to tell. She remained hopeful that inspiration would strike soon.

Myla struck a match and dropped it on top of *Blood Moon Rising.* Flames engulfed the painting, and then quickly spread to Steven Alenzo's clothes. She stepped back from the flames, knowing that the cabin would soon be reduced to a pile of ashes.

Myla took the blank canvas with her when she left.

CHAPTER 10

THE LANDLINE PHONE WAS ringing when she returned to her apartment in Manhattan. Her hands were full, and she didn't bother trying to answer the phone. Her cellphone was still on charge in the bedroom. Because cellphones were also tracking devices, she had not taken hers to the Catskill Mountains.

The landline stopped ringing.

Myla set the crossbow down on the coffee table. Then she mounted the blank canvas on the easel that was set up in her living room.

She was still dressed in the camouflage clothes. She emptied her side pockets of the gun, the spare arrows, and the hunting knife. She put those on the coffee table next to the crossbow. Then she took the compass and the binoculars from around her neck and set those on the coffee table, too.

The landline began ringing again. Myla lifted the cordless phone from its cradle. For once, she didn't cringe when she saw her sister's name and numbers on the screen. Instead, she simply pressed the TALK button. "Hello, Marlow."

"Hi Myla. I'm sorry to bother you, but Nick wants to know if you've had a chance to get his old photo albums down from the attic yet."

"Not yet."

"I see. Well, are you doing anything now? I could come over and help you look for them, if you're not too busy."

Suddenly, inspiration struck. Myla picked up the hunting knife and looked over at the blank canvas. "Actually, I'm not doing anything right now. I'm not busy at all. Why don't you both come over?"

"Seriously?"

"Yes."

"Both of us? Are you sure?"

"Absolutely. I think it's time we all three buried the hatchet."

"Oh, Myla, it's so great to hear you say that! I'll tell Nick, and then we'll both come over right away. You're my sister, Myla, and I'm always going to love you. No matter what."

"I love you too."

Myla pressed the END button. Then she returned the phone to its cradle.

She was excited. The handle of the hunting knife seemed to be tingling in her hand.

She crossed the room and stood before the blank canvas on the easel. The canvas would not be blank for long.

Myla smiled. She finally had a story to tell.

PART TWO: COUNTDOWN TO OBLIVION

CHAPTER 1

CHUCK PARKED HIS CAR behind The G-Spot and went inside. He ordered a glass of whiskey at the bar. Then he found an empty table in front of the stage and had a seat.

All around him, men cheered and whistled at Ginger on the stage as she twirled her pigtails and the tassels hanging from her nipples in perfect time to the music of the live band on the smaller stage to her left, but Chuck sipped his whiskey in silence. The band wasn't too bad (especially for a Tuesday night), and the whiskey wasn't watered down at all. And though the men around him would hoot and yell for anything in a G-string, Ginger was a bona fide knockout.

Her performance ended, and Ginger went backstage. As the band kept playing, another dancer took the stage.

A few minutes later, Ginger sat down at Chuck's table, sipping a beer.

He handed her a hundred-dollar bill. "Where's Jenny?"

She put the money in her bra. "Haven't seen her."

"Since when?"

Ginger shrugged.

He gave her another hundred. "Since when?"

"Saturday night."

He sipped his whiskey and handed her another hundred. "Who did she leave with?"

"Who else?" Ginger said. "She left with Jericho."

Son of a bitch, Chuck thought. *I'll fucking kill him.* "Do you know where they went?"

Ginger nodded.

He gave her another hundred-dollar bill. "Where did they go?"

She told him.

Chuck finished his whiskey and stood up.

"Do you know where that is?" Ginger asked.

He nodded. "I do. Thank you."

He left.

CHAPTER 2

CHUCK BOUGHT A GUN out of an older car's trunk in a bad neighborhood on the east side of town. A skinny Black man (friend of a friend) with demonic eye contacts sold it to him. It was a Glock 19. The man told him it was untraceable. Chuck gave the man some cash and that was that. He checked to see if the semiautomatic was loaded while the man drove away, and he saw that it was.

Chuck thought maybe he was doing the world a favor by buying the gun. If he hadn't bought it, perhaps it would have ended up in some crackhead's hand, and possibly aimed at some Hindu storekeeper from India who just wanted to send his kids to college. This way, only Jericho would get shot, and the Hindu guy could keep saving up money for his children's education.

Chuck fired up a cigarette, took a drink of whiskey, and drove out of the parking lot. His destination was only a hundred miles away. He could do the speed limit and be there in less than two hours, easily. He didn't know if his daughter was still alive or if she was dead, but either way, he was going to make Jericho pay.

HE STOPPED FOR GAS halfway there at a ramshackle filling station and went inside. The attendant—a middle-aged white man with thick forearms—had a lot of amateurish, green-ink tattoos.

"Surprised to find a place open at this hour," Chuck said, "in the middle of nowhere."

"And I'm not surprised that you're surprised," the attendant said. "Fucking idiot."

Chuck had the gun in the waistband of his jeans. The demon on his left shoulder told him to shoot the man in the face; the angel on his right shoulder told him not to.

Chuck paid cash for the gas, then went outside and pumped.

He drove away and parked his car about a hundred yards down the road. Then he took his jacket off, put a ski mask on, and walked back to the store.

The attendant stood out front, smoking a cigarette.

Chuck looked around; he didn't see any cameras anywhere. Keeping to the shadows at the otherwise empty parking lot's perimeter, he quietly made his way to the side of the store, then quickly approached the man and put the gun to the back of his head. "One wrong move and you're a dead man. Do you understand me?"

"Yes."

Chuck forced the man into some woods beside the store, and then shoved him to the ground.

The attendant looked up at him. "Money's in the store, man. I don't have any."

"I don't want your goddamn money," Chuck said. "I want an apology."

"An apology?"

Chuck raised the ski mask, revealing his face. "Yes. The demon wants me to kill you, but the angel is telling me to let you live. So, if you apologize for calling me an idiot, I won't blow your fucking brains out right here in these godforsaken woods."

"Okay, man. I'm sorry. Jesus Christ. I'm sorry for calling you an idiot."

Chuck nodded. "Okay. Apology accepted. Now give me your fucking wallet."

"My wallet?"

"Yes."

"Man, I already told you: I don't have any money."

"I don't want your goddamn money. I want your driver's license."

"My driver's license?"

"Yes. And I'm in a hurry here, so unless you want me to shoot you in the fucking face—"

"Nah, man. Fine." The attendant retrieved his wallet from his back pocket and proffered it to Chuck. "Here. Take my fucking wallet."

Chuck took the wallet with his left hand while keeping the gun aimed at the attendant's face. It was an old leather wallet and he found the license in the top card slot. He tossed the wallet onto the ground and held the license up in the moonlight. "Buster Jones? Seriously? That's your real name?"

"Yeah. Why? You got a problem with my name?"

"No, Buster. I do not. Anyway, I just showed you how easily someone could kill your dumb ass for being rude to them. So, from now on, be nice. You'll have to get a new driver's license, though, because I'm keeping this one so I don't have to memorize your address. And if the cops come asking me any questions about this incident, I'll find your ass and kill you no matter what the angel says. Do you believe me?"

"Yes."

"Good for you. Have a nice life."

CHAPTER 3

CHUCK WEPT UNTIL HE began seeing highway signs for his destination. He kept a box of tissues on the passenger's seat and a plastic bag on the floorboard in which to put his trash. He often got too emotional when he drank, but tonight, the booze was not the reason for his tears. He wept because the demon kept telling him that his daughter was dead; that Jericho had already killed her, and that Jenny most certainly was not in Heaven.

The angel said nothing, and if Hell existed, Chuck wanted to send Jericho there for whatever it was he had done to Jenny.

SHE HAD BEEN A good kid, his Jenny. Chuck was of the opinion that kids got meaner with each generation, and kids these days were not only meaner than ever—most of them were downright Satanic. Jenny, however, had basically been a decent human being and a halfway good-hearted person. But then her mother died when Jenny was ten, and nothing was ever the same after that.

Jericho got her into drugs and alcohol when she was in seventh grade, and it was all downhill from there.

Jenny stopped going to school altogether when she was in tenth grade. Chuck never made her go back, even though he knew her mother would have wanted him to. He felt better having her home with him. He had been hoping things would work out for the best. They didn't, of course, and every bit of that was Jericho's fault.

When Chuck reached the small town that was his destination, he didn't immediately go to the abandoned church. First, he went to an all-night Walmart and purchased a hunting knife.

Chapter 4

THE BUILDING LOOKED AS if it hadn't been used as a church for quite some time. All the windows were boarded up, and a broken cross still jutted from the eaves.

Chuck took a drink of whiskey. Then he got out of the car with the gun in one hand and the hunting knife in the other. He heard a dog barking down the road as he made his way to the front porch. Firelight flickered through the crack between the door and its jamb. He put an ear to the door and listened. Whispers hissed from the interior, and he heard people grunting and moaning inside. Chuck wondered how many people were currently living in the abandoned church. Pushing the door open, he smelled the burning-plastic stench of crystal meth. Taking a deep breath, Chuck stepped inside.

He saw several faces in the light of candles burning in scattered coffee cans. All the faces looked the same to him: sick, skeletal-thin, and riddled with scabs. A woman—slick with sweat—looked up at him and opened her mouth, but she didn't say anything. All of her teeth were gone. A glistening rope of drool hung from her lower lip. The pews were gone (undoubtedly used as firewood), so the meth-heads were sprawled out on filthy blankets strewn all over the floor. Chuck didn't count them, but he guessed there were twenty at least. A few of them fucked on the floor like feral dogs, oblivious to Chuck and their fellow tweakers.

A skinny kid with greasy hair and black rings beneath his eyes looked up at Chuck, and grinned. Most of his teeth were gone. "Want me to suck your dick?"

"I'm looking for Jericho," Chuck said.

"Jericho won't suck your dick, but I will."

Chuck looked around. The stench of crystal meth and unwashed flesh made him gag. He covered his mouth and his nose with a hand and walked away.

He found Jericho at the front of the room where a podium had once stood. Chuck hadn't seen him in a while, but he recognized him immediately. Jericho was pulling his pants up. He had just finished having sex with a girl who looked about as wasted as he did. Jericho turned around and fired up a cigarette, looking at Chuck.

"I'll be damned," Jericho said. "The news just broke an hour ago. Did you come to say goodbye before the world ends?"

Chuck raised the gun. His son was out of his mind and speaking nonsense. He aimed the gun at Jericho's face. "Where is she?"

"Who?"

"Your sister," Chuck said, "you dumb son of a bitch. Jenny. Where the fuck is she?"

Jericho shrugged. "Jenny's downstairs."

"Downstairs?"

"Yes. In the basement."

"What the fuck's she doing in the basement?"

"Taking care of Trinity."

"Trinity?"

"Yes."

"Who the fuck is Trinity?"

"Some woman's little girl. I don't remember the woman's name. She died a couple of nights ago, and now Jenny's taking care of Trinity. Not that it matters now, of course. Nothing goddamn matters anymore."

"What the fuck are you talking about?"

Jericho approached his father, smiling, and opened his arms as if to embrace him. "Haven't you heard, Pops? The whole world's coming to an end. So you should let your son give you a hug."

Then Jericho lunged for the gun. He wrapped a hand around Chuck's wrist and drove a knee into his stomach.

Chuck's arm shot upward and he squeezed the trigger reflexively, sending a bullet into the ceiling. The knee to his stomach had stunned him, but he didn't release his grip on the knife in his other hand. He brought the hunting knife up and rammed its blade deep into Jericho's throat. Jericho didn't have time to scream, but he did make a few gurgling sounds as his hands went up to the knife's handle.

Chuck yanked the blade out. A thick gout of blood erupted and splashed onto the floor. Then Jericho hit the floor and died in a spreading pool of blood.

"Holy shit!" someone yelled. "Motherfucker just killed Jericho!"

Chuck—still holding the gun and the hunting knife—turned around and braced himself for an onslaught of vengeful meth-heads, but none came. He asked the nearest one, "Which way to the basement?"

The wretched man pointed at a door to Chuck's left.

Chuck went to the door and opened it. A stairway descended into darkness. Smoke rose from below, and with it came the burning-plastic stench of crystal meth. He saw firelight flickering from beyond the bottom of the stairway.

Chuck glanced back and saw that none of the meth-heads were even looking at him. Then he went downstairs into the church's basement.

He found Jenny and a little girl sitting on the concrete floor of a small room. Candles burning in coffee cans provided illumination.

Jenny looked the same as she did the last time he had seen her: on the skinny side, but otherwise still attractive. She was a twenty-year-old woman who—despite her addiction—had thus far managed to avoid the outward physical ravages of crystal meth. She had a needle stuck in her arm, and she recognized him immediately. When she smiled, Chuck was pleased to see that she still had all of her teeth. "Hi, Dad," she said. "How did you find me?"

"Ginger," he said. "She told me you left the club with your brother the other night."

Jenny nodded and pressed the plunger, injecting herself with liquid meth.

Chuck looked down at the little girl beside her. She appeared to be eight or nine years old. She was filthy, and her clothes were ragged. Scabs covered her face. She was so thin she reminded him of one of those kids in the old photos of the starving Ethiopian children, except she was white. She was smoking ice by holding a lighter against a lightbulb converted to a meth pipe.

"Are you Trinity?" Chuck asked her.

She looked up at him, and Chuck could see her clearly in the candlelight. She had blue, haunted eyes with dark rings all the way around them. She didn't say anything; she just stared at him and kept smoking ice out of the lightbulb.

"Yes," Jenny said. "This is Trinity. Her mother died a few nights ago."

Chuck nodded. "I know. Your brother told me."

Jenny pulled the needle out of her arm and lit a cigarette. "You talked to Jericho?"

"Yes."

"Is he still upstairs? He should have been back down here already."

Chuck shook his head. "Jericho's not coming back."

"What are you talking about?"

"Jericho's dead."

"Dead?"

"Yes. He tried to kill me, so I damned near cut his head off."

Jenny cocked her head, and it looked to Chuck that it dawned on her for the first time that her father held a gun in one hand and a hunting knife in the other. Her eyes appeared to go blank for a second, and then an expression of absolute horror seemed to transform the features of her face. "Oh my god," she said. "You fucking killed him?"

Chuck nodded. "I did. And I'm not a goddamn bit sorry about it."

Jenny—sitting on a blanket—put the syringe down and abruptly stood up. "But Dad, you don't understand! Jericho had the meth! We don't have any! Jericho had the meth in his pocket!"

"Oh," Chuck said. "Well, yes, I suppose that would be problematic for you. Want me to go get it?"

Jenny nodded rapidly, puffing her cigarette. "Yes. Please. Jesus fucking Christ. I just hope it's still there."

Chuck turned around and hurried back upstairs.

He found Jericho's corpse exactly where he had left it. Two male tweakers stood over the body, looking down at it, probably trying to decide whether to go through Jericho's pockets. He raised the gun and quickly approached the tweakers. "Get away from him," Chuck said, "or you motherfuckers will be just as dead as he is."

The two tweakers scurried off into the shadows.

Chuck found the meth in Jericho's pocket. The ice was in a sandwich bag. The bag was so full that shards of crystal had poked through in several places. He put the bag in his jacket's interior pocket. Then he grabbed Jericho's wallet and headed back down the stairs, returning to the candlelit room.

"Was it still there?" Jenny asked, pacing the room while Trinity still sat on the floor.

Chuck nodded. "I got it. I also grabbed this." He proffered Jericho's wallet.

Jenny accepted her brother's wallet. "Thanks." She took the money out of the wallet and then tossed the wallet aside. She put the money in her pocket. "Some of that cash was mine, anyway. Not that it matters now, of course. Supposedly, everyone on Earth will be as dead as fried chicken by tomorrow night."

"So what the hell exactly is going on?" Chuck said. "Did someone declare nuclear war while I wasn't looking?"

Jenny shook her head. "No. At first they were saying an asteroid was coming, but now they're saying it's something worse."

"They?" Chuck said, making air quotes with his fingers—despite the fact that he still held the gun in one hand and the hunting knife in the other.

Jenny nodded. "Yes. They."

"Who the fuck are *they?* Who the fuck is saying that?"

"Goddamn *everybody,* Dad. Jesus fucking Christ. Don't you ever get online?"

Chuck shrugged. "Not often. And what the fuck could be worse than a goddamn asteroid?"

"I don't know," Jenny said. "My phone is almost dead. I need to get to a place with electricity."

"So let's go home," Chuck said. "We can be there in two hours."

Jenny shook her head. "No, Dad. That's not my home anymore. Whenever I'm there, I see Mom's ghost everywhere. Can we just get a room? There's plenty of hotels in this town. I'll pay for it."

"Sure, if that's what you wanna do. And don't worry about the money. I'll pay for the room."

"Thanks, Dad. I just need to grab my stuff."

A suitcase and a duffel bag sat on the floor. Jenny picked the syringe up and put it in the duffel bag. "Give me your pipe, Trinity," she told the little girl.

Trinity handed Jenny the lightbulb that had been converted to a meth pipe.

Jenny put the meth pipe in her duffel bag. Then she put the duffel bag in her suitcase. She closed the suitcase and picked it up.

Then she asked Chuck, "Can I carry the meth? I would feel better with the meth in my pocket."

"Sure." He gave her the bag of meth.

She looked at it, nodded, and put it in her pocket. Then she looked down at the little girl. "Come on, Trinity. We're leaving."

Trinity stood up, and Jenny grabbed one of her hands.

They left.

CHAPTER 5

CHUCK DROVE. JENNY RODE next to him on the passenger's side. Trinity rode behind them in the back.

"Can we go to Walmart first?" Jenny said. "I need to get a few things for Trinity. I'll be fast."

"Sure." Chuck drove them to the same Walmart in which he had purchased the hunting knife.

They went inside. The store looked like most stores do at four o'clock in the morning: all but empty except for overnight stockers.

Jenny grabbed a shopping cart, but—because she was holding Trinity's hand—she asked Chuck, "Will you push this?"

Chuck had left the hunting knife in his car; the gun was in the waistband of his jeans at the small of his back. "Sure."

Jenny bought some soda, a few snacks, a toothbrush, toothpaste, body wash, deodorant, shampoo, conditioner, an outfit, and some tennis shoes for Trinity.

They left.

Chuck drove them to a motel down the road—a ranch-style building with one long row of rooms, and no second floor. The room doors all faced the parking lot. According to the sign, vacancy was available. The office was lit up.

He parked in front of the office, killed the engine, and turned to Jenny. "You wanna wait out here with her, while I go get us a room?"

"Sure," Jenny said.

Chuck got out and went inside the office. Ten minutes later, he got back in the car. "It's already four in the morning. Since checkout time's eleven, I booked the room for two days."

He moved the car and parked in front of their room. The three of them got out and went inside.

There were two queen-sized beds in the room.

Chuck, holding Jenny's suitcase, said, "I'll take the bed by the window." He put her suitcase on the floor next to the bed nearest the bathroom.

Jenny shrugged. "Works for me." She set the bags containing her purchases from Walmart on the floor beside her suitcase.

"I gotta go grab my whiskey," Chuck said. "Be right back."

He went outside. The bottle in his car was halfway empty. The one in the trunk hadn't been opened yet. He grabbed both and went back inside.

Jenny and Trinity were sitting on their bed. Jenny had already put her phone on charge. She had also already removed her duffel bag from the suitcase. She took the lightbulb that had been converted to a meth pipe from the duffel bag and handed it to Trinity.

A nightstand by their bed was bolted to the wall. On the nightstand sat a phone and a phone book. Jenny took the syringe and a bottle of water from her duffel bag and set them on the nightstand. Then she put the phone book on her lap and used it as a tray for the bag of crystal meth.

Chuck sat down at the table by the window. He took a few shots of whiskey while Trinity smoked meth and his daughter prepared some for injection. Jenny used the old crush-and-shake method that he had seen many of his friends (most of whom were now dead) use over the years: crush the ice into powder, mix it with water in the syringe, and then shake until the powder is gone.

After injecting herself with meth, Jenny got up and grabbed some of the Walmart bags from the floor. Then she told Trinity, "Come on, little girl. You need a goddamn bath."

Trinity put her meth pipe on the phone book. Then she rose from the bed and followed Jenny into the bathroom.

Chuck got up with his bottle of whiskey and found the remote control. He turned the TV on and sat down on his bed. He flipped through several channels before stopping on a news station. His gun—digging into the small of his back—became uncomfortable. He withdrew it and set it next to him on the bed.

He took a few drinks of whiskey and watched the news. According to numerous reports, riots were breaking out all over the planet in reaction to a forthcoming apocalypse. He was so drunk he had to keep putting one hand over an eye to keep from seeing two TVs.

He took a few more drinks. Soon, he was unconscious.

CHAPTER 6

CHUCK DID NOT SLEEP long. When he woke up, the little girl lay sleeping to his left on the other bed. To his right, his daughter sat at the table by the window, staring at her phone. A cartoon was now playing on the TV.

He stood up, grabbed his bottle, and took two drinks of whiskey.

"Nice nap?" Jenny asked.

He shrugged. "I guess. I'm fucking starving. I should have grabbed some food while we were at Walmart."

"So, have some of Trinity's snacks. She didn't eat any of that crap I bought her. She took a bath and pretty much passed out."

Chuck looked over at Trinity. She lay sleeping in the new clothes Jenny had purchased. Her hair was still wet. "She looks like a fucking skeleton. I'm not eating her food. Mind if I smoke some of your meth?"

Jenny lowered her phone and looked up at her father. "I didn't know you smoked meth."

Chuck took a drink of whiskey. "I smoked it once, before you were born, so that had to have been over twenty years ago. I *loved* the goddamn buzz, but it took me like three fucking days to come down from the shit, so I never smoked it again. But now? Fuck it. I'll smoke the shit."

Jenny nodded at the bag on the table. "Knock yourself out."

Chuck took a drink and set his bottle on the table. "Be right back."

He went into the bathroom and emptied his bladder. He washed his hands and splashed some water on his face. He put some toothpaste on a finger and brushed his teeth. Then he went back out and sat down across from Jenny at the table.

She handed him the pipe and a lighter. "Already packed it for you," she said.

Chuck smoked the crystal meth, and the ice hit him immediately. His drunkenness was gone, replaced by a soaring euphoria. The high was like a cocaine buzz, but a whole lot more intense.

Finished with the pipe, he set it down and fired up a cigarette. They were in a nonsmoking room, so they were using disposable cups half-filled with water to flip their ashes and put their cigarette butts in.

"Sorry about the cartoon," Jenny said. "I changed channels for Trinity. Want me to put it back on the news?"

Chuck shrugged. "Whatever you wanna do."

"Then I'll just leave it," Jenny said, "in case Trinity wakes up. The news is a bunch of bullshit, anyway."

Chuck took a drink of whiskey. "What time is it?" The blinds and curtains over the window were closed.

Jenny looked at her phone. "Almost seven a.m. The president's supposed to address the nation at eight."

Chuck cocked his head. "At eight o'clock in the morning? Isn't that awfully early for a presidential address?"

Jenny put some meth and some water in her syringe. Then she began shaking it. "It's the end of the world, Dad. All of us are supposed to be gone by nine o'clock tonight."

Chuck rolled his eyes. He had a hard time believing the world was coming to an end, but a lot of people apparently believed it was true. He remembered seeing news reports of people rioting overseas before he had passed out a few hours ago. He took a drink of whiskey. "Did you ever find out what the fuck's supposed to happen?"

Jenny injected herself with meth. "No. Just like everyone else, I've heard everything from asteroid impact to alien invasion. But I've got a friend back home who says he knows for sure what's coming, and he told me that if we go there, he can show us."

"A friend?"

"Yes. He messaged me while you were sleeping."

Chuck put his cigarette butt in one of the plastic cups. "Who's your friend?"

"Kyle Orban." Jenny pulled the needle from her arm and set it down. "Smart dude. About your age. He used to teach physics at the university, but he got fired."

"For what?"

"Not sure. I heard something about a scandal involving underage girls, but I'm pretty sure he was never charged with anything."

"How do you know him?"

Jenny shrugged. "We used to date, but now we're just friends."

Chuck took a drink. "He's my age, and you used to date him?"

Jenny lit a cigarette. "He's like you: he looks a lot younger than he is. And you bang chicks my age all the time, so fucking save it."

Chuck couldn't argue with that. "What's his name again?"

"Kyle Orban."

"And you think this Kyle Orban knows what the fuck he's talking about? That he can show us what's supposedly coming to destroy the planet?"

Jenny nodded. "I wouldn't doubt it. I mean, he was drunk when he messaged me, but that's nothing new. He's like you: total alcoholic. But the dude definitely knows what the fuck he's talking about."

Chuck took another drink. "You wanna go see him? We can be there in two hours."

"Sure. But first, I think we should watch the presidential address."

She grabbed the TV remote and began changing channels, stopping on one of the major networks.

"—reporting to you live from the press briefing room in the White House," an attractive blonde woman was saying on the screen. "The president's spokesperson has informed us that the address is now less than an hour away, so we'll be staying live on the air until the address takes place. By now, most of you probably know the nature of the address, and that it relates to an impending apocalypse. Thus far, however, all the information we've received regarding the apocalypse has been unverified, so basically we don't know anything more than you do. So stay tuned. Again, we'll be staying live—"

Trinity grabbed the meth pipe and a lighter from the table. Neither Chuck nor Jenny had seen the little girl rise from her bed.

"Pipe's empty," Chuck told her.

"Here, Trinity," Jenny said. "Give me the pipe. I'll load it for you."

Trinity handed Jenny the meth pipe. Jenny loaded the pipe and gave it back.

Then the three of them spent the next forty-five minutes getting high until an image of the presidential seal filled the TV screen.

The image of the presidential seal cut away to a shot of the president sitting behind his desk in the oval office. He was flanked by an American flag and a blue flag bearing the presidential seal. He wore a black suit with a white shirt and a blue tie. His forearms were at rest on the desk. His hands were clasped.

The president sat forward and cleared his throat. "My fellow Americans, today it is my duty to deliver the worst possible news to you and the rest of the world. I've spent the past two days debating if I should even tell you what I'm about to reveal. Many on my staff and even my wife advised me not to do so. They believe that it would be better for the people of this great nation to spend the last few hours of their lives in blissful ignorance of the doom headed their way from the blackness of outer space."

Chuck glanced over at Jenny. She was looking at Trinity. The little girl was staring at the TV.

"Sixty-five million years ago," the president continued, "an asteroid struck this planet and killed the dinosaurs. Today, mankind meets a similar fate. The object approaching us now, however, is not an asteroid. We honestly don't know what it is. We *do* know that it is far, far larger than the asteroid that killed the dinosaurs, that it's moving with incredible speed, and that the certainty of impact with Earth is one hundred percent. There is no possibility of a miss. This is an extinction-level event. Today is the last day of life on planet Earth."

Chuck took a drink of whiskey. Jenny put some meth and some water in her syringe. Trinity just kept staring at the TV.

"The main reason I decided to go ahead with this address," the president said, "was to let you know how much time is left. All the scientists I've spoken to agree that we have about twelve hours from right now until impact, which puts the end of everything at approximately sometime between eight o'clock and nine o'clock tonight. I hope that each of you will spend the remaining time with your loved ones, and find whatever peace you possibly can. So long, America. And farewell, planet Earth. May God have mercy on our souls."

The image of the presidential seal reappeared.

Jenny grabbed the remote. She turned the TV off and looked at her father. "Are you ready to go see my friend?"

Chuck nodded. He then stood up, took a drink, and grabbed his other bottle. "Yes. Let's hit the road."

CHAPTER 7

CHUCK DROVE. JENNY CONTROLLED the stereo from the passenger's side. Trinity smoked crystal meth in the back. As far as Jenny and Chuck knew, the little girl had never been to their hometown. For most of the two-hour trip, they listened to various news stations and talk radio. According to numerous reports, riots were breaking out and people were looting stores all over America.

"And it's still early," Chuck said. "It's only gonna get worse as the day goes on."

They arrived at Kyle Orban's house shortly past ten a.m . He lived in a quiet neighborhood of stucco and clapboard bungalows constructed many years ago. Most of those homes undoubtedly provided more charm than space, but Kyle Orban's house was one of the largest in the neighborhood. A two-car garage was attached to the house. Both garage doors were down. The driveway was empty.

Chuck parked in front of the garage door farthest away from the house and killed the engine. "Nice place."

"His parents owned it," Jenny said. "It became his when they died. They left him some money, too. I'm pretty sure he hasn't worked since getting fired from the university."

The three of them got out of the car. Chuck had finished his first bottle a few miles back, so he only carried one bottle now—which he hadn't opened yet. Trinity held a lighter in one hand and her meth pipe in the other. Jenny left her suitcase in the trunk; her duffel bag hung from one of her shoulders. She looked up into the bright blue sky and shielded her eyes. "Hard to believe something's gonna come out of that sky and kill us in about ten hours."

"I know you said your friend's an alcoholic," Chuck said. "But what about drugs?"

Jenny lowered her gaze from the sky. "Kyle takes drugs."

"So he won't mind us sitting around doing meth until the world ends?"

"No. Trust me: Kyle loves crystal meth. Us having meth will make him happy. Come on. Let's go see if he's awake yet."

Jenny led the way. Chuck followed the two of them up the front walkway and they climbed three steps to the porch. Jenny pressed a button by the doorframe. They heard a doorbell ring inside the house. Moments later, a man opened the door.

"Hi, Kyle," Jenny said. "Did we wake you?"

Kyle was tall and thin. His long gray hair was tied back in a ponytail. He wore a bathrobe and held a cocktail glass. "No," he said. Then he looked at Chuck. "You must be Jenny's father."

Chuck nodded. "Name's Chuck."

Kyle sipped his drink. "Nice to meet you, Chuck." Then he looked down at Trinity. "And what's your name, little girl?"

Trinity didn't even look at him.

"This is Trinity," Jenny said. "She doesn't speak much."

Kyle took another drink. "It's nice to meet you, Trinity."

Again, she refused to acknowledge him.

Kyle stepped back and opened the door a little more. "Come on in, people. We'll have ourselves a countdown to oblivion."

He led them through the foyer into a living room furnished with a sofa, a loveseat, and a couple of armchairs. Bookshelves lined the walls. Empty bottles and an overflowing ashtray sat on the marble-and-granite coffee table. "Have a seat," Kyle told them. "And pardon the mess. It's rare that I have company. Be right back."

He left the room and returned with a trash bag. Chuck, Jenny, and Trinity were sitting on the sofa. Jenny was in the middle. Her father sat to the right of her and the little girl sat to her left. Kyle put the empty bottles in the trash bag. Then he emptied the ashtray and carried the trash away. When he came back, he sat down on the armchair closest to Trinity's side of the sofa.

Trinity set her meth pipe on the coffee table and looked at Jenny expectantly. Jenny pulled the bag of meth from her pocket and put some in the pipe. Trinity (already holding a lighter) picked the pipe up, put a flame to the meth, and started smoking.

Retrieving the syringe and the bottle of water from her duffel bag, Jenny prepared some meth for injection. Then she stuck the needle in a vein and pressed the plunger.

Chuck cracked open his fresh bottle of whiskey. He took two drinks and then looked at Kyle. "Jenny said you told her you can show us what's coming to kill us."

Kyle sipped his cocktail. "I can. And I will. But first, I wanna get high." He produced his own pipe from a pocket of his bathrobe—a little glass pipe that still had some marijuana in its bowl. He dumped the marijuana into the large ceramic ashtray. Then he pointed at the bag of meth next to it on the table and asked Jenny, "May I?"

She nodded. "Knock yourself out."

Kyle packed his bowl with meth and started smoking it. "Goddamn," he said, after only a couple of hits. "This shit's dynamite."

Chuck smoked some meth out of Trinity's pipe while Kyle finished smoking his.

Then Kyle set his bowl down on the coffee table and rose from the armchair. "Okay, people. It's time to show you my satellite-surveillance chamber. Follow me."

The three of them rose from the sofa. He led them out of the living room, down a hallway, and into another large room on the other side of the house.

Two of the walls in the room were longer than the other two. On one of the longer walls was an immense screen about the size of most screens in a cinema. A map of planet Earth was projected on the screen. Cloud formations were superimposed on the map. Green lettering was superimposed on the cloud formations.

"What do the green letters mean?" Trinity said.

Those were the first words Chuck had heard the little girl speak.

"Weather conditions," Kyle said. "Worldwide." He sat down at a control console in front of the massive screen. "And all these other lights," he added, referring to the blue, red, yellow, and white lights blinking steadily on the screen, "indicate the current positions of numerous satellites."

"What do the satellites do?" Trinity said.

"A lot of them just handle electronic communications," Kyle said.

Trinity's eyes kept sweeping over the lights across the screen. "So all those satellites are just for cellphones?"

"Oh no," Kyle said. "I mean, yes, a lot of them *are* just used for cellphones, TV, internet, and radio. But others are used for astronomy, meteorology, oil exploration, domestic surveillance, international espionage, all kinds of stuff."

"Who owns the satellites?" Trinity said.

Kyle shrugged. "Government agencies. Military services. Public corporations. U.S. and foreign businesses. Doesn't really matter to me, though, because I can access and use just about every satellite on that screen without the legitimate owners even knowing that their systems have been invaded."

Chuck took a drink of whiskey. "Are you serious?"

Kyle nodded. "Check this out." He pushed a button on the console, and the map of planet Earth vanished from the screen. In its place, an actual satellite view of New York, Pennsylvania, and New Jersey appeared. The borders of those three states were overlaid in orange lines because their boundaries would have been otherwise difficult to define when seen from orbit. Then he pushed another button and the camera zoomed all the way in on a license plate. An image of the license plate filled the entire screen. Kyle glanced up at Chuck. "Look familiar?"

Chuck shrugged. "I don't know my fucking plate number. Is that mine?"

Kyle pushed a button and the camera zoomed out a bit, revealing an image of Chuck's car parked outside in front of the garage.

Chuck took a drink. "So whose satellite *is* that, anyway? Goddamn NASA's?"

Kyle finished his cocktail. "Yes, actually. It belongs to NASA."

Chuck shook his head. "I'll be damned."

Jenny said, "So what the fuck's coming to kill us?"

There was a keyboard on the console. Kyle tapped a few keys, and the image on the screen was replaced by a view of glittering stars in outer space. He clicked a mouse beside the keyboard to highlight a fuzzy, grayish shape among the stars. The smudge of gray had pinpricks of light in it. "That's what's coming to kill us."

"What is it?" Trinity said.

"You tell me," Kyle said. "What does it look like to you?"

"A silver dragon," Trinity said.

Kyle scratched his chin. "Interesting."

Chuck took a drink. "It looks like a cosmic cloud."

"To me," Jenny said, "it looks like a little swirling galaxy." She turned to Kyle. "But you're the goddamn genius, so what the fuck is it?"

He shrugged. "I don't know. No one does. I do have a theory, however, and I think Trinity was pretty close when she said it looks like a dragon. But I don't think it's going to breathe fire and destroy us. Instead, I think it's going to eat us."

Jenny looked at Kyle. "Eat us? So you think it's alive?"

He nodded.

She put a hand on a hip. "And you think it's going to eat the entire planet?"

He nodded again. "Actually, I think it might eat most of the solar system."

Chuck took a drink. "No offense, dude, but I think you're stupid."

"None taken," Kyle said. "And you're certainly not the first person to think that. But we just started seeing these things yesterday, so no one's had enough time to figure out *what* the hell they are."

"Wait a second," Jenny said. "*Things?* As in plural?"

"Yes. They began appearing yesterday all across the Eridanus Void."

"The what?" Jenny said.

"The Supervoid of Eridanus. A space of absolute nothingness, about a billion light years across. For years, the CMB couldn't find anything there."

Chuck said, "What's the CMB?"

"It's a map of the cosmic microwave background, which is basically electromagnetic radiation from the early stages of the universe. Anyway, for years, we couldn't find anything in that massive space, and then, yesterday, these things just started popping up all the way across the supervoid. Strange, to be sure. Inexplicable, actually. But not an imminent threat to us, because the Eridanus Void is billions of light years away. Fast forward a couple of hours, however, and one of those things is practically right outside our door. In just a few hours from now, it kicks in the door and kills us all."

Chuck took a drink. "So there's no chance it misses us? Or maybe just passes right on by?"

Kyle shook his head. "None. I don't think you understand how big it is. Go ahead and take another look at it."

Chuck, Jenny, and Trinity all three looked up at the screen. The swirling gray smudge was already bigger than it had been just a few minutes ago.

"Those pinpricks of light inside it," Kyle said, "are bigger than Jupiter."

Chuck and Jenny looked at Kyle with their mouths open. Trinity just kept staring at the screen. Jenny said, "No fucking way."

"And I think," Kyle added, "that those pinpricks of light are its eyes."

Jenny looked at her father. "Let me hit that whiskey." He handed her the bottle, and she took a drink. Then she took another drink and gave the bottle back.

Kyle stood up from the control console. "I wanna show you something. Follow me."

He led them to a computer workstation in a corner of the room. Beside the computer workstation was a light table. On the light table were several large photographic negatives of the thing from outer space that was coming to kill them. Also on the light table were a few little handheld magnifying glasses.

"Go ahead," Kyle said. "All three of you. Grab a magnifying glass and tell me what you see."

Chuck, Jenny, and Trinity each picked up a magnifying glass and began examining the photographic negatives.

"I see tentacles," Trinity said.

Chuck said, "I see a goddamn mouth."

"Me too," Jenny agreed. "And teeth. Jesus Christ. Look at those fucking teeth."

"That mouth is big enough to swallow stars," Kyle said. "And those teeth are the size of planets and moons."

"And the eyes!" Jenny said. "Those eyes look absolutely demonic! What the hell *is* this thing?"

"I don't know," Kyle said. "They just appeared out of nowhere all over the cosmos yesterday. My best guess is that they came from another dimension, and now they're traveling through our spatial plane, devouring whole constellations, and leaving nothing but cosmic voids in their wake."

Chuck took a drink. "Well, we've only got about eight or nine hours left, and even though I'm high on this goddamn meth, I'm fucking starving."

"I'm hungry, too," Jenny said. "I haven't eaten in about a week. You think anybody's still delivering food on the last day of existence?"

"Doubt it," Kyle said. "But I could make us all a big pot of spaghetti. How does that sound?"

Chuck took another drink. "Sounds good to me."

"Same here," Jenny said.

Kyle turned to Trinity. "How about you, little girl? Are you in the mood for some spaghetti?"

Trinity shrugged.

"Her mother died a few nights ago," Jenny told Kyle. "I haven't seen her eat anything since."

"So it's settled then," Kyle said. "I'll make us all a big pot of spaghetti."

The four of them went back into the living room and did some more crystal meth. Then Kyle went into the kitchen and made a pot of spaghetti. Soon thereafter, the four of them ate spaghetti, bread, and potato chips at the table in Kyle's dining room. For dessert, they each had a Popsicle.

"I'm tired, now," Chuck said, after the meal's conclusion. "Think I might kick back and catch a little shut-eye."

"Me too," Jenny agreed. "I'm probably gonna nod off for a bit."

Kyle rose from the table. "I normally do the dishes right away, but not today. I am, however, going to take a shower. Just crash wherever you want. Make yourselves at home." He turned around and walked out of the dining room.

Chuck, Jenny, and Trinity went back into the living room. The bag of meth was still on the coffee table. Trinity sat down on the floor, put some meth in her pipe, and started smoking it.

Jenny stretched out on the sofa and closed her eyes. "Doubt I sleep long," she said. "Just need a nap."

Chuck found a bedroom down the hallway. He went inside and closed the door behind him. He stretched out on the bed and took two drinks of whiskey. Moments later, he was asleep.

CHAPTER 8

"DAD! WAKE UP!" *JENNY'S voice.* "Dad! Wake up! Trinity's missing!"

Chuck opened his eyes. Jenny stood next to the bed, looking down at him with wild eyes and wild hair.

Chuck got up and took a drink of whiskey. "She's gotta be around here somewhere."

"She's not," Jenny said. "I looked all over the house. And I can't find Kyle, either."

Chuck took another drink, remembering the uneasy feeling he got every time he saw the way Kyle looked at the little girl. He also remembered Jenny telling him that Kyle had been fired from the university because of a scandal involving underage girls.

"I'm still drunk," Chuck said. "I need to smoke some meth and get my head straight."

They went into the living room. Trinity's pipe lay on the coffee table next to the bag of crystal meth. They sat down on the sofa. Chuck smoked some meth while Jenny shot herself up.

Then they heard a little girl scream.

Jenny looked at her father. "Was that Trinity?"

The scream had sounded like it came from below.

"I don't know," Chuck said. "Does this place have a base-ment?"

"I think it does. There's a door in the kitchen, but it's locked, so I couldn't open it."

She got up, and Chuck followed his daughter into the kitchen. According to the clock on Kyle's microwave, the time was 4:06 p.m.

"Is that clock right?" Chuck said.

Jenny pulled her phone out and looked at it. "Yes. Didn't think I would sleep that long. We have about four hours until the end of the world."

She led him to a door between a corner of the room and the kitchen sink. The door could be secured from their side by a padlock, but it was not. The padlock was locked through the hole in the staple on the wall by the doorframe, but the hasp attached to the door wasn't latched over the staple.

Chuck tried to turn the doorknob; it was locked from the other side. "Want me to pick the lock?"

"You know how?"

"Of course I do." He drew his gun from the waistband of his jeans at the small of his back. Then he raised a leg and kicked in the door. It crashed open against the wall by a stairway descending into a basement. "Ta-da."

A weird stench hit them immediately.

"Jesus Christ," Jenny said. "What the fuck is that smell?"

"I don't know." Chuck raised his gun. "It smells like lemons and ammonia." He started down the stairs.

Jenny followed her father into the basement.

When Chuck flipped a light switch at the bottom of the stairs, a series of lightbulbs on the ceiling came to life.

"Oh my god," Jenny said.

Chuck said, "Jesus fucking Christ."

The basement ran the length of the entire house, and a long hallway divided it down the middle. On both sides of the hall-way, secured by chains attached to cuffs around bones and links in the cinderblock walls, the corpses of maybe fifty or sixty underage girls hung in varying stages of decay.

"I had no idea Kyle was a goddamn monster," Jenny said. "No wonder he was always burning incense and spraying air freshener upstairs."

"But still," Chuck said, "the smell should be worse than this. Son of a bitch must use some kind of a witch's brew to keep the stench to a minimum."

Then they heard a little girl start screaming from somewhere down the hallway. They followed the screams down the hall to the last door on the left. The door was made of wood. They heard a final bloodcurdling scream, followed by silence. Chuck didn't bother trying to open the door; he raised his gun and simply kicked it in. Jenny entered the room behind him.

Kyle—naked—stood in the middle of the room with his back to them. He held Trinity's severed head by the hair in one hand and a hacksaw dripping blood in the other. Her decapitated body lay on the floor. Blood still spurted from her neck stump, spreading all over the concrete.

Kyle turned around and faced them. His penis was fully erect. He smiled. "The drugs made her hideous, but pain made her beautiful. She's flying with all the angels now."

Chuck aimed his gun at Kyle's face. "Tell the devil I said hello." Then he shot him right between the eyes.

"I wanna go home," Jenny said. "I wanna see Mom's ghost before the world ends."

Chuck nodded. "Me too."

They left.

CHAPTER 9

CHUCK DROVE. JENNY RODE next to him on the passenger's side. According to the dashboard clock, the time was 5:31 p.m.

Chuck's house was on the other side of town.

Rush-hour traffic in the city always moved at a frustrating pace, but this evening, in some places, it was at an absolute standstill. They saw stalled cars everywhere. The streets and sidewalks were becoming more and more clogged with people who abandoned their vehicles and took off walking. On the radio, they heard numerous reports of people committing murder and suicide in the streets.

By the time they reached their destination, it was after six o'clock.

"Two hours left," Jenny said. "Approximately." She sat down on the living-room sofa, placing the bag of meth on the coffee table.

Chuck sat down beside her and took a drink of whiskey. "Did you bring Trinity's pipe?"

"Yes." She pulled the pipe from her duffel bag, along with her syringe.

For the next two hours, they talked and did a lot of crystal meth. They also listened to rock and hip-hop music. Chuck kept looking at the clock on his stereo; Jenny kept looking at her phone.

The sun began to set around eight o'clock. Twilight entered the world and the light withdrew. Jenny turned off the music and they listened to events on the radio. The announcer promised to keep broadcasting right up until the end.

They heard a sound like thunder. Jenny scooted closer to her father and pulled him into an embrace. He took a drink of whiskey. Then he put an arm around her shoulders.

Jenny looked up at a portrait of her mother hanging on the wall. "Do you think we'll see her?"

"I don't know. I hope so."

"Me too."

Soon thereafter came the sound of a roaring wind. Jenny closed her eyes. Chuck saw a fast blur of motion beyond the window.

Then blackness.

PART THREE: BLACK CAT BONES

CHAPTER 1

A DAY AFTER SHE turned nine, Alicia found her dragonfly dead inside its pickle jar. *Don't cry,* she thought. *Nine years old is too old to cry.*

Alicia pulled the dragonfly out of the jar and held it up. "Goodbye, Kobalt." Opening her bedroom window, she tossed him down to the sidewalk below.

Already dressed, she brushed her teeth in the bathroom across the hall. Then she grabbed the pickle jar and carried it downstairs.

Thankfully, she didn't see her mother (or her mother's current boyfriend, Alan) while crossing the living room. Opening the front door, she descended the steps to the sidewalk in front of the four-story brownstone.

With the pickle jar cradled in one arm, she hoped to avoid the attention of the older boys gathered across the street. School would be starting soon, and she knew they had a lot of meanness stored up after being away from their studies for so long. Fortunately, she made it to the end of the street without attracting their attention.

Soon thereafter, a very tall, thin, black man approached her at a crosswalk. He stopped in front of her and glared down. He wore grimy pants and an Army field coat with a hood over his head and gloves on his hands despite the sweltering summer heat, and he carried a walking stick so big he could rest his chin on it. "Hi, little girl. Why you carrying that pickle jar around? You looking for black-cat bones?"

Looking up, Alicia shielded her eyes from the sun with the hand not holding the jar. "Black-cat bones?"

"Yes. The bones of black cats. Is that what you're looking for?"

"I'm looking for pets," Alicia said. "Why would I be looking for the bones of black cats?"

"There's a lot of dark magic in black-cat bones, little girl. What's your name?"

"Alicia. And I know who you are."

"You do?"

"Yes. You're Darnell Staples."

"How do you know that?"

"My mother told me."

"Do I know your mother?"

"No. We just moved here. But we see you walking around everywhere. My mother says you're a homeless schizophrenic."

"Is that right?"

"It's what she told me."

"I'm not homeless. This whole city is my home."

"She says you used to be smart, but you took a white girl to a party a long time ago, and some racists put a bunch of acid in your drink and fried your brain."

Darnell shrugged. "I don't remember that. Would you like to see my home?"

"You said the whole city was your home."

"It is. And since you just moved here, I can give you a tour of the city. Come on."

They took off walking, exploring the city for about an hour, talking about a little bit of everything. Alicia liked Darnell immensely. He was definitely crazy, and smelled like an animal, but he was nice and told fascinating stories.

More time passed. They kept walking. Darnell did most of the talking, and Alicia loved listening to him speak. After a while, she noticed that gulls no longer circled overhead. She also noticed that she could no longer smell the scent of the nearby ocean. Realizing that she was now far from her mom's apartment, she suddenly began feeling hungry.

Looking up at a sign above a donut shop, Alicia asked Darnell, "Do you have any money?"

"A little bit. But I have to save my money for gasoline. I don't need money to get some donuts, though. Come on."

She followed him inside. The place was nearly empty. Fluorescent lightbulbs flickered in the ceiling.

Darnell pointed up. "Black-cat bones," he said. "In the light fixtures. Making the lightbulbs flicker."

A teenage girl behind the cash register nodded at Darnell. "We have a box of donuts for you, but you'll have to go around back to get them."

"Thank you," Darnell said. "God bless you."

Alicia followed him outside, then around the building to the back.

Another employee (a teenage boy) opened the rear entrance and handed Darnell a box of donuts. "Here you go, Mr. Staples. Have a nice day."

"You too," Darnell said. "God bless you."

The boy closed the door.

"That's awesome," Alicia said, "that they give you free donuts."

Darnell shrugged. "The manager doesn't like me, but the people who work here do. Come on. Let's go to the park and eat our donuts."

Carrying her empty pickle jar, she followed him to a nearby park. Darnell carried the donuts and his walking stick.

Alicia said, "Where do you wanna sit?"

Darnell shrugged again. "You pick."

She led him to the park's edge, where they sat on the ground in the shade beneath a tree.

The day was warm, and the sun was shining. Joggers were out, and a few people walked dogs. Two kids tossed a Frisbee in the otherwise empty playground in the distance.

"Don't you get hot?" Alicia said. "Wearing all those clothes?"

Darnell shook his head. He had not removed his hood. His walking stick now leaned against the tree, but he still wore his gloves while eating a donut. "No," he said. "I'm always cold."

Alicia captured a praying mantis and put it in her pickle jar.

"New pet?" Darnell asked her.

"Yes."

"Those things are evil."

"I know. I want a tarantula, but I don't see one."

"I see tarantulas all the time," Darnell said.

Alicia's eyes widened. "You do?"

"Yes. Next time I see one, I'll catch it and save it for you."

"Thanks!"

They ate an equal number of donuts until the box was empty.

Then Darnell stretched out on the ground. "I'm ready for a nap."

"Me too."

Alicia lay on the ground next to her pickle jar, staring at the praying mantis.

Soon, she was asleep.

CHAPTER 2

ALICIA OPENED HER EYES to see the sun going down. Sitting up, she saw that Darnell was already awake. He stood leaning against the tree, holding her pickle jar and studying the praying mantis in the blood-red light of sunset.

"Lots of bad mojo associated with these things," he told her. "Almost as bad as black-cat bones."

"Should I let it go?"

He nodded. "That's probably for the best."

"So release it," Alicia said.

He did, and the praying mantis slowly crawled away.

"How much you want for this pickle jar?" Darnell said. "I had a few, but all mine broke. I need a jar to keep my gasoline in."

"You can just have it," Alicia said. "I can always get another one."

Darnell nodded, putting the pickle jar in one of the deep pockets of his Army field coat. "Thank you. God bless you."

"Is there a zoo around here?" Alicia said.

"Yes. Not too far from here."

"How much does it cost to get in?"

"I don't know. I can get us in for free, after they close. But you probably have to be home soon, don't you?"

"No."

Darnell cocked his head. "You don't?"

"No."

"How old are you?"

"Nine. I turned nine yesterday."

"Nine years old, and you don't have a curfew?"

"No. My mother's a junkie. She never even knows when I'm away."

"What's she addicted to?"

"Heroin. She shoots it up with needles. Her boyfriend's a junkie, too. His name is Alan, and I absolutely hate him. Sometimes, Alan rapes me."

"He rapes you?"

"Yes, but only when he can find me. I'm very good at hiding from him. When he *does* find me, I just go to other places in my mind."

Darnell looked away. "The mind's an awfully big place. There's a lot of places people can go and hide inside their minds."

They watched the sky grow dark in silence.

Later, they walked to the zoo, which was already closed when they got there. Circling the property's perimeter, Darnell led Alicia to a cut in the fencing, where they waited by the fence until the main lights along the thoroughfare went out and the overnight lamps came on.

"Most of the staff will be leaving soon," Darnell told her. "Then no one else will be in there but the cleaning crew and the security guards. If anyone sees us, we'll just run. The security guards are lazy. They won't chase us."

They watched a few cars leave through the front gate to their left. Then they squeezed through the opening in the fence and walked up the deserted pathway.

The pavement was rutted. Alicia saw cracked paint and faded signs everywhere. She smelled tar, rancid food, urine, and animal feces.

"All these animals look so sad," she said. "They don't know how to take care of their pets here."

"These aren't pets," Darnell said. "They're puppets for the public's entertainment. These animals are broken creatures who've been enslaved for exhibition. The whole thing is terrible and grotesque."

"Yes," Alicia said. "It's horrible. I wish I could take them all home as pets. Well, not to my mother's apartment, of course, but to a farm somewhere. I wish I had a farm that I could take them to and keep them all as pets. That would be a wonderful life."

"I wish I could burn this place to the ground," Darnell said, "but I don't have enough gasoline. Actually, I don't have *any* gasoline. I need to go get some."

"To start fires at night? To keep yourself warm?"

"Yes."

"I'm ready to leave," Alicia said.

Darnell nodded. "There's a pet store not far from here that sells exotic pets. You wanna go see if they're open?"

"Yes!"

"They may be open, but they may not be. Sometimes, they're open all night, and sometimes, they're closed for days. Never can tell about them. It's also a pawn shop. Do you know what a pawn shop is?"

"Of course. My mother's a junkie, remember? She's always pawning her stuff."

They left the zoo, climbing back out through the hole in the fence, then walked to a place called PETS 'N PAWN a few blocks south. The lights were off, and Alicia saw a CLOSED sign on the door.

Darnell shifted his walking stick from one hand to the other. "Oh well. We can try again tomorrow."

Alicia shrugged. "Okay. Do you think they have any tarantulas?"

"Maybe."

They turned and headed back toward downtown, cutting through multiple alleyways in the darkness. Alicia heard strange grunts in the shadows. She also heard whispers, cackled laughter, and empty bottles rolling on the pavement.

"I'm thirsty," Alicia said.

Darnell pointed to a corner store down the street. "Come on. I need to get some gasoline. I'll buy you something to drink."

In the store, Alicia grabbed a bottle of apple juice, and Darnell grabbed a bottle of wine. Using cash, he paid for their drinks and prepaid for enough gasoline to fill the pickle jar.

Outside, at the pumps, he filled the jar with gasoline and shoved it into one of his deep pockets. Then they took off walking around downtown.

Darnell finished his wine before Alicia finished her apple juice, even though his bottle was bigger than hers.

"One of my friends vanished the other night," he said. "A witch."

"Your friend's a witch?"

"Yes. She was messing around with some black-cat bones, and something came out of the darkness and snatched her. But I have a key to her apartment, and she might have some tarantulas in there, if you wanna go look around."

Alicia's eyes widened. "Yes! I'd love to go look around!"

Darnell nodded. "Okay. Let's go."

She followed him to a brick-faced apartment building not far from her mother's apartment. Entering the building, they took an elevator up to the seventh floor, then Darnell led her to apartment 7B.

Unlocking the door with a key, he opened it, and they stepped into a narrow central hallway. He closed the door behind them and locked it.

Alicia saw four doors on either side of the hallway. She followed him to the last door on the left, which was painted black. Darnell opened the door, and they entered a windowless room.

The walls, floor, and ceiling were painted black. Fluorescent lightbulbs in the ceiling provided illumination. There was no furniture in the room, and Alicia saw little white bones all over the floor.

"Black-cat bones?" she asked him.

Darnell nodded. "Yes. This is the room she disappeared from."

"How do you know?"

"Because I was with her when it happened," he said. "And look," he added, pointing toward a swirling red dot on one of the walls. "There's the portal."

"The portal?"

"Yes. She told me that she had opened a portal to other dimensions, and the other night, something reached out and grabbed her. Took her away. I saw it happen. The portal was black the other night, though—blacker than the walls of this room. But tonight, the portal is red."

As Alicia watched, the swirling red dot on the wall grew larger. Soon, it resembled a vertical whirlpool, but full of blood-red gases and smoke instead of water. It also looked like a tunnel.

Then something large, blazing, and shaped like a hand reached out, grabbed Darnell, and yanked him into the tunnel.

After Darnell vanished, the portal shrank into a swirling dot on the wall again.

"Darnell?" Alicia said, looking around the now otherwise empty room. "Can you hear me?"

Silence.

Alicia searched the apartment for tarantulas. She didn't find any.

CHAPTER 3

ALAN STOOD WAITING FOR Alicia in the living room when she returned to her mother's apartment. Her mother lay passed out on the sofa.

Alan approached her. "Where the fuck you been?"

"Looking for pets," Alicia said.

He grabbed her by the hair. "I'll give you a fucking pet."

He dragged her into her bedroom, closing the door behind them and locking it, and then slammed her onto the bed.

Alicia closed her eyes and went to another place in her mind.

CHAPTER 4

THE NEXT DAY, SOON after waking up, Alicia tiptoed to her mother's bedroom door, which was slightly ajar. Pushing it open, she saw that both her mother and Alan were still asleep.

She entered the room.

On Alan's side of the bed, his jeans lay on the floor next to his boots and his wadded-up socks. A wallet attached to a chain jutted from a pocket of his jeans.

Quietly approaching the wallet, Alicia bent over and opened it: the wallet was full of money—which didn't surprise her; Alan, in addition to being a junkie, was also a drug dealer. Her mother always ended up dating drug dealers.

Alicia took half the money and put it in her pocket.

Turning to leave the room, she saw Alan's handgun on a nightstand. She didn't know much about guns, but she knew enough to aim and pull a trigger. She also knew that Alan's gun was a "nine" (whatever that meant), because he talked about his gun all the time.

She tiptoed over to the gun and picked it up. The gun—black—wasn't heavy and felt like it was made of both metal and plastic. GLOCK 19 AUSTRIA 9x19 was engraved on one of its sides. Aiming the gun at Alan's face, she resisted an urge to pull the trigger.

Setting the gun down, Alicia left the apartment and took off walking.

CHAPTER 5

THE NIGHT BEFORE, ALICIA had not locked the door when leaving the witch's apartment, and it was still unlocked today when she returned. Opening the door, she entered the witch's apartment, then walked down the hallway and stepped into the last room on the left.

The blood-red portal—still a small dot—continued to swirl on one of the walls, and everything looked the same except for one: there were less bones on the floor than the night before. Last night, there had been many; today, only a few.

Had they been sucked into the tunnel when Darnell got abducted?

She couldn't remember.

Before she left, Alicia picked up two of the black-cat bones and put them in her pocket.

CHAPTER 6

PETS 'N PAWN WAS open when she got there. The pawn
section was in the front, so she assumed that the pets were
in the back. Other than a grimy, mean-looking man behind
the cash register, the place was empty.

Alicia said, "Do you have any tarantulas?"

"No."

"What all do you have?"

"Pets are in the back."

Alicia went into the back and discovered that there weren't
a lot of pets *in* PETS 'N PAWN. She saw a few dogs and cats
in cages; a couple of hamsters; a rabbit; several fish in filthy
tanks that flanked the cages.

And then she saw a human head floating in an aquarium on
the floor. Alicia dropped to her knees for a closer inspection.

The head featured the face of a beautiful woman. The
woman's eyes were closed, and her long orange hair looked
like flames burning in the water. If the head had been severed
from a body, it must have been a clean cut, because Alicia
saw no signs of decapitation along the bottom of the neck.
The neck just ended smoothly in a perfectly fine, slightly
rounded stump—as if the head had never been connected
to anything.

And then the eyes opened and looked up at her. Alicia thought the woman's eyes were the most beautiful green eyes she had ever seen.

The woman smiled and then transmitted a word: *Hello.*

The smile never changed because the lips never moved; Alicia heard the voice in her mind.

I'm Cora. What's your name?

Alicia didn't know if Cora had vocal cords or not, but she believed it would be impossible to speak without lungs, and Cora certainly had no lungs or anything else that a regular person would have below a neck. She assumed that Cora's brain received oxygen from the water, and that she had somehow learned to communicate telepathically.

"I'm Alicia," she said. "It's nice to meet you."

Cora's smile never left. *It's nice to meet you, too. Take me home with you and we'll always be together.*

Alicia shrugged. "Okay. I'll be right back."

She returned to the front, where the grimy man still stood behind the cash register. "How much for Cora?"

He shot her a look. "Huh?"

"The head in the aquarium back there. On the floor. Come on. I'll show you."

He followed her into the back.

Alicia pointed to the head in the aquarium. "Her name is Cora. How much do you want for her?"

"One hundred dollars. You give me a hundred dollars, and you can take her home—tank and all."

She handed him a hundred-dollar bill. "And how much for that wagon out there?"

There weren't many toys in the pawn shop, but Alicia had seen two bicycles and a little red wagon when she walked in.

"The wagon is a hundred dollars, too," the man told her.

She gave him another hundred-dollar bill. "Will you put her in the wagon for me?"

He went out front, got the wagon, and pulled it into the back. Unplugging the aquarium, he picked it up and set it in the wagon. "Enjoy your head."

"Thank you," Alicia said.

She left.

CHAPTER 7

WHEN ALICIA PULLED HER wagon up to the steps in front of the brownstone, a neighbor who lived in the building stood checking his mailbox by the sidewalk.

"I'll give you a hundred dollars," she told him, "if you'll carry this aquarium upstairs for me."

He shot her a look as if she were crazy, cocking his head. Then he shrugged and picked up the aquarium. "Whatever."

Carrying the wagon, Alicia followed him up to the fourth floor, where she paid him in front of her mother's door after he put the aquarium back in the wagon.

"Can you wait here for a second?" she asked him.

"I guess."

Opening the door, she didn't see her mother or Alan in the living room.

Alicia asked the man, "If I pull the wagon into my bedroom, will you set the aquarium on my desk for me?"

"I suppose I can."

She pulled the wagon into her bedroom, and the man followed. After she cleared her desk, the man lifted the aquarium out of the wagon and placed it on her desk.

Then he left.

Parking the wagon in front of her closet, Alicia sat down on the chair at her desk, facing Cora. "How do you like your new home?"

Cora's smile brightened her green eyes even more. *I love it here, Alicia. It's beautiful. And so are you.*

They conversed until Alicia's eyes grew weary.

She stretched out on her bed and fell asleep.

CHAPTER 8

THE NEXT MORNING, ALICIA woke up when Alan grabbed her feet and dragged her off the bed. Her head smacked the floor.

"A *fish tank?*" he yelled, standing over her. "You stole my money to buy a fucking *fish tank?*"

Her mother entered the room. "Calm down, Alan. I'll make her return the fish tank. She'll take the fish tank back, and then she'll get your money back."

"You're goddamn right she will." Alan returned his gaze to Alicia. "If I don't have my money by tomorrow, I'll kill your stupid octopus and throw that fish tank out the window."

Alan and her mother left the room.

You'll have to kill him, Cora transmitted, not smiling. She didn't appear to be angry at all; she just looked sad. *If you don't kill him, he's going to kill me.*

"I know," Alicia said. "He thinks you're an octopus."

She got dressed, brushed her teeth, then left and walked downtown to the library.

She got online at one of the public computers, typing Glock 19 into the search browser. Then she spent an hour reading information about Alan's handgun. She knew his gun would be loaded, because she had heard him say, "*fifteen in the clip, one in the chamber,"* many times, and apparently Glocks had no safety switches, so she didn't have to worry about that.

Alicia rose from the computer.

Because she still had plenty of money, she decided to go to a restaurant and treat herself to breakfast.

CHAPTER 9

ALICIA SPENT THE ENTIRE day away and then went home late that night.

In the living room, Alan and her mother lay passed out on the sofa. Alan snored. Her mother slept with a needle stuck in her arm.

In the kitchen, Alicia grabbed a pair of the disposable gloves her mother often used when washing dishes and put them on. Then she went into their bedroom and grabbed the gun.

She took the pistol into the living room, where Alan and her mother still lay sleeping. Placing the gun to the back of Alan's head, Alicia pulled the trigger, blowing his brains out the front of his skull. The gunfire was deafening, but her mother never even stirred.

She returned the gun to Alan's nightstand. Then she went to the bathroom and flushed away the disposable gloves.

Back in her own bedroom for the first time since that morning, Alicia discovered that Cora was now gone. Alan had replaced her with an orange octopus, which currently sat serenely at the bottom of the aquarium.

He must have killed Cora, she thought, *before I blew his brains out.*

Crying, Alicia stretched out on the bed and closed her eyes. It was a long time before she fell asleep.

CHAPTER 10

THE NEXT DAY, HER mother shook her awake. "Alan's dead. Someone shot him in the head. The police will think it was me. Hell, it may have *been* me. I'm high as a kite, and I don't remember anything. We have to get out of here."

Alicia sat up on the bed. "Where will we go?"

"My father has a cabin in the woods, about two hours upstate. He only uses it during hunting season, but he keeps the electricity on all year long—and the water. He also keeps it stocked with canned foods. I have a key, so we can just hide out there for a while, until I figure out what to do. Pack your suitcase. We're leaving."

"What all should I pack?"

"Just a few of your favorite outfits, mainly. You don't have to take a lot of clothes. Alan left a briefcase full of cash beneath the bed, so we'll just buy some new clothes later on. He also left a briefcase full of heroin, so I don't have to worry about that. Don't forget your toothbrush. Oh, and pack some books, so you don't get bored. I know how much you like to read."

Her mother left the room.

Rising from the bed, Alicia glanced over at the aquarium—in which the octopus now lay dead. Most of the water had leaked from the tank and was now a puddle on the floor. Apparently, the octopus had somehow removed the aquarium's drain plug sometime during the night.

She got dressed, putting on the same pants she had worn the past few days—in a pocket of which she still carried the black-cat bones.

Alicia went across the hall and brushed her teeth. Wrapping her toothbrush and the toothpaste up in a clean towel, she took the towel with her back into her bedroom. She put the towel in her suitcase, along with some favorite clothes and some favorite books. She also packed her notebooks, a few pencils, and a couple of pens. Closing the suitcase, she set it down in the hallway.

Then she went into her mother's bedroom, where her mother stood packing her own suitcase, which lay on her bed next to two open briefcases. One of the briefcases was full of cash; the other was full of heroin. Alan's pistol lay on the nightstand where she had left it.

"We should take the gun," Alicia said. "Just in case."

"You're right." Her mother grabbed the pistol and shoved it into the briefcase full of heroin. Opening the nightstand, she withdrew a box of bullets and put it in the briefcase full of cash. Closing both briefcases, she finished packing her suitcase.

Then they hit the road.

CHAPTER 11

TWO HOURS LATER, ON a dirt road in a forest, their car broke down.

"Fuck!" Alicia's mother yelled, managing to pull to the side of the road before the car completely stopped. She popped the hood and got out.

Moments later, she got back in. "The serpentine belt broke. We'll have to walk the rest of the way. Fortunately, the cabin's only about a mile up the road. But first, I have *got* to shoot up. I'm too sick to walk anywhere right now."

She quickly prepared a syringe in the driver's seat. Then she injected herself with heroin. Soon thereafter, she sat with a faraway look in her eyes, smiling dreamily. "Okay. I'm ready." She popped the trunk, and they got out.

Taking the handgun from the briefcase it was in, Alicia's mother shoved it into the waistband of her jeans, then grabbed her suitcase and the briefcase full of heroin. Alicia grabbed her suitcase and the briefcase full of cash. They took off walking.

The day was warm. The sky was blue. They saw no signs of civilization from the dirt road while walking through the forest.

They walked in silence for a while, then Alicia's mother pointed to a cabin straight ahead. "There it is."

Several hills loomed behind the cabin, and a tower stood perched atop the tallest.

"What's that tower for?" Alicia said.

Her mother shrugged. "Airplanes, probably. Or maybe cellphones. I used to date a guy whose job was to climb those towers and change the lightbulbs."

"Sounds like a scary job."

"Yeah, but they paid him pretty good to do it."

Soon, they reached the cabin.

Alicia's mother had a key, but she didn't need it, because the lock on the front door had been broken. Setting her suitcase down on the porch, she withdrew the gun from her waistband. "Someone broke in. You wait here. I'll go in first and check it out."

She went inside. Moments later, she returned and picked up her suitcase. "There's no one in there. Come on in."

Alicia followed her mother inside. She looked around. The cabin was small, consisting of a kitchenette, a bathroom, a bedroom, and a living room that comprised the bulk of the place.

Her mother sat down on the couch. "You can have the bedroom. I'll sleep out here in the living room." She prepared a syringe and injected herself. Soon thereafter, she passed out.

Alicia walked around the cabin, checking it out, then sat down next to her mother and opened a book.

Perhaps an hour later, her mother woke up. "Are you hungry?" she asked Alicia.

"Yes. I haven't eaten since yesterday. I thought you said your father keeps food here."

"He does."

"There's no food here. I already checked."

Her mother got up and walked into the kitchenette, searching for food. She found the clean dishes, the silverware, the pots and pans, the can opener, and the running water that Alicia had already found, but there was nothing to eat. "Great. The burglars must have stolen all the food. Anyway, the nearest town's about twenty miles away, and our car's not going anywhere, so I guess I'll have to call a tow truck."

She withdrew her phone from her back pocket. "Fuck! My phone's dead. I hope I remembered to pack a goddamn charger."

Returning to the living room, she searched her suitcase for a charger, but didn't find one. "Oh, my god. I totally forgot to bring a phone charger. We are so fucked."

Alicia put her book down. "Do you think your father has one here in the cabin somewhere?"

Her mother shook her head. "I doubt it. I don't even think he *has* a cellphone. But we can look."

They searched the cabin. They did not find a phone charger.

Her mother prepared another syringe and injected herself, getting wasted on heroin and staying that way.

Alicia drank plenty of water.

Several days passed before she ate. She stopped counting at eight.

Chapter 12

There was no TV in the cabin, but Alicia's mother kept the old transistor radio in the living room tuned to an FM rock station.

Eventually, Alicia got sick of the music. One night, while her mother lay passed out, she switched to AM radio and scanned the dial, stopping when she heard a man's familiar voice—a voice she recognized even before he said the words, *"Black-cat bones."*

Alicia hadn't seen him since he had been yanked from the witch's apartment, but somehow Darnell Staples was talking on the radio, rambling about black-cat bones.

And then she remembered that she had some black-cat bones in her pocket. She had been wearing the same pants for a couple of weeks.

Dogs eat bones, Alicia thought, *and so can I.*

She took the bones from her pocket and ate them. Nothing in her life had tasted better. She could have eaten more, but a couple of bones were better than none.

For dessert, she drank a glass of water.

Then she listened to Darnell on the radio:

" . . . hard and troubled times for us all, so whatever it is you're going through out there, just know you're not alone. All of us are going through these hard and troubled times together.

And whatever it is you're doing to cope with all these black-cat bones, more power to you. Once upon a time, when I was young, I used to pray to God for guidance when I was lost, but it's been a long time since I've prayed for anything. And I'm not going to lie to you: before I got to where I'm sitting right now, there were times when all I wanted to do was climb a clock tower with a high-powered rifle and start killing people just to put them out of their misery. But I didn't do it, and neither should you, even though I know that many of you feel the same way I did. But I'm not lost anymore, and hopefully, you won't be lost for too much longer. So again, whatever it is you're doing to cope with all these black-cat bones, more power to you. I'll be back later."

Alicia fell asleep on the floor in front of the radio.

CHAPTER 13

SHE WOKE UP HUNGRY. Her mother had changed the radio back to a rock station.

Rising from the floor, Alicia found her mother surprisingly awake. Her mother sat upright on the couch. A dark blanket covered her from the waist down, despite the heat of the cabin's interior.

Perhaps she's getting sick, Alicia thought.

She knew that her mother had to be just as hungry as she was. She also knew that her mother was very high by the look in her eyes.

"There's some meat on the stove," her mother told her, "but you'll have to cook it. You know how to cook, don't you?"

"I know how to make French toast and scrambled eggs."

"Meat's no different. Just cook it over the heat until it's done."

Alicia cocked her head. "Where did you get the meat?"

Her mother pointed to the pistol on the coffee table, which lay next to a bloody steak knife and a bloody butcher's knife. "I shot a squirrel while you were sleeping. I already ate my share. The rest is yours."

She then stuck a needle in her arm.

Alicia went into the kitchenette—where a voice inside her mind told her not to eat the meat; to throw the meat away; to eat the black-cat bones instead.

But I already ate all the bones, Alicia thought.

She found more bones in her pocket nevertheless.

Tossing the meat outside, Alicia ate the bones.

The black-cat bones were delicious.

CHAPTER 14

THAT NIGHT, WHILE HER mother slept, Alicia switched to AM radio and listened to Darnell Staples. The radio didn't pick up many AM stations to begin with, and the few that it did pick up were fuzzy at best, but Darnell's voice came through as clearly as if he were sitting next to her in the cabin's living room.

"The forest has many voices," Darnell said. "The buzzing of insects. The wings of bats. The mad howling of wolves. Occasionally those voices go quiet and I can hear the more terrifying voices that lurk beneath the normal nocturnal noise. The forest whispers to me, telling me of things I never even knew existed, sharing secrets older than planet Earth itself, and I write these secrets down, as I have been ordered by the cosmos to do so."

Alicia heard his microphone picking up the sound of papers being shuffled around on a desk.

Then he said, "I will broadcast these secrets when I can, whether or not anyone is even listening, but writing the secrets down is crucial, and I *have* been writing them down, as did the chosen few who came before me. Their words are here in this ancient studio with me, and I have been reading them, and I will continue to read them until someone else comes along to take my place. I'm surrounded by manuscripts stacked from the floor to the ceiling, and I've been busy composing my own manuscripts ever since my arrival here not long ago. Although perhaps I shouldn't have used the word arrival, for I didn't simply arrive at this place. I was snatched from the city by a force from another dimension and brought to this ancient studio in the forest."

Alicia heard more papers being shuffled. She also heard a few sips of something being swallowed. Then Darnell started talking again.

"This studio is full of both old and modern radio equipment, but it's also filled with canned food, weapons, and ammunition. There's enough beer, liquor, and wine here to last several lifetimes. I don't know who pays for the water and the electricity, and I don't suppose I need to know. Maybe no one pays for it. Maybe it's just here and always will be. Who knows? Not me. Not yet, anyway. But the forest tells me secrets, and I'm listening. I'm also signing off for now. I have work to do. If you're listening, keep doing whatever you're doing to deal with all this madness and the black-cat bones."

Alicia switched the radio back to an FM station and fell asleep.

CHAPTER 15

SUNLIGHT THROUGH THE WINDOW woke her up. Hungry, Alicia rose from the floor and stretched.

Her mother, already awake, sat on the couch with the blanket over her legs. She looked awful. She also looked incredibly high. "There's some more meat on the stove. Just needs to be cooked. I killed us another squirrel while you were sleeping."

Her mother stuck a needle in her arm.

Alicia found more bones in her pocket and ate them.

CHAPTER 16

ALICIA SPENT THE DAY reading. Her mother spent the day injecting herself with heroin. While her mother drifted in and out of consciousness, Alicia sat and worried about her mother. Her mother's health had deteriorated the past few days, and now she looked like she was dying. When she staggered into the bathroom several hours after nightfall (shivering despite the cabin's heat and the blanket she was wrapped in), it was the first time Alicia had seen her rise from the couch in a couple of days. Then her mother staggered back to the couch, injected herself with heroin, and passed out.

Alicia switched to AM radio and listened to Darnell Staples.

"I haven't been here long," Darnell said. "It's early in my mission, and I'm excited by the things that I've discovered here. When I first got here, and started flipping through some of the manuscripts that surround me, I noticed that many of the dates went back several hundred years, and I realized that this was not just a broadcast booth, but a library of arcane sorcery and ancient information. I'm talking about highly advanced learning. Mind-boggling mathematics. Quantum physics combined with previously unknown history and a staggering understanding of magic and inter-dimensional travel."

Alicia heard papers being shuffled around.

"I speak," Darnell said, "of some of the things that I have read in these manuscripts, but I also speak of what the forest has whispered to me. I'm talking about magicians and divinities. I'm talking about creation and eternal life. And we most certainly *were* created, by the way. We didn't just emerge from some primordial soup and evolve into what we are today. Oh, no. We were created through *true magic*, and tiny sparks of that true magic reside within us all. In some of us more than others, certainly, but it resides within us all nevertheless."

Alicia heard him pause to take a drink.

"We don't even know what we're capable of," Darnell resumed. "We built the pyramids thousands of years ago, and we still don't know how we did it. And we most certainly were *not* created to live our entire lives as blind and as ignorant as insects. And so the work must go on, and it *will* go on. The truth must be told, and it *will* be told. The lost knowledge given to us from elsewhere—the outer technology; the sacred geometry; the true magic—will not only be reacquired, but *expanded* upon, and we will not only rise to those glorious dimensional heights that we once knew as a young civilization, but we will *surpass* them. I'm talking about liberation. I'm talking about transcendence. I'm talking about eternal life. That is the mission. With that, I'm signing off. I have work to do. If you're listening, be vigilant. And for God's sake, beware those black-cat bones."

Alicia switched to FM radio and fell asleep.

CHAPTER 17

THE SOUND OF SOMETHING crashing in the bathroom woke her up. Rising from the floor, Alicia didn't see her mother on the couch. She also didn't see her mother's blanket.

She walked to the back of the cabin. The bathroom door was closed. She tried to open the door, but it was locked. "Mother? Are you okay?"

"Be right out," her mother said.

Moments later, her mother opened the door, wrapped in the thick blanket. She looked horrible. She looked like an animated corpse.

Alicia saw blood on the floor. "Mother, you're bleeding."

"I fell. It's no big deal." Her mother staggered into the living room.

Alicia followed.

Her mother sat down on the couch. "I killed another squirrel while you were sleeping, so there's some meat on the stove, if you're hungry."

"Thank you, Mother."

"You're welcome." Preparing a syringe, she injected herself with heroin and passed out.

Alicia walked into the kitchenette. She saw the uncooked meat, but didn't eat it. Instead, she found more bones in her pocket and ate those.

Returning to the living room, Alicia looked for Darnell on the radio, but didn't find him. *He's probably working on one of his manuscripts,* she thought.

Alicia went into the bedroom and closed the door. Grabbing a book to read, she also grabbed a notebook and a pen.

She then spent the day as she had spent most of her days recently: either reading, sleeping, or writing about her dreams.

CHAPTER 18

ALICIA WOKE UP AND looked out the bedroom window. Night had fallen. She loved how she could see far more stars in the sky from a forest than from a city.

She got up and went into the living room. She didn't see her mother on the couch, nor her blanket. She then went to the bathroom door, but it was closed. She knocked. "Mother? Are you okay?"

"Yes. Do you need in here?"

"No. Just checking on you."

"I'm gonna take a bath."

"Okay, Mother. Do you mind if I change the radio station?"

"No. Go right ahead."

Alicia went back into the living room. She switched to AM radio and heard Darnell's voice. She then sat down on the floor, and listened:

". . . but none of that matters anyway, for there is magic and wisdom here, not the terror and the madness they want you to believe. Anything that they don't understand, they call it madness. But it is *not* madness. It is the intended progression of humanity. They try to tell us that doing what we were placed here to do by our creators is evil, that slicing open the divine fruit of knowledge is wrong, but it is *not* evil. It is *not* wrong. And right now my mission and the mission of others in the service of truth is the most important work that humanity is performing on planet Earth. And I, and others like me, will continue to wage war against those who oppose this information."

Alicia heard him pause to take a drink.

Then he said, "Before I got here, I spent a lot of my time think-ing about all the despair, terror, and savagery that humanity inflicts upon itself. But now, even when I'm working—which, I'll admit, is pretty much always—I'm thinking about the paintings by Jan Vermeer, and the music of Beethoven, and the transcen-dent works of literature by humanity's greatest authors. I used to think about how matter is nothing more than energy that's been brought to a screeching halt, and about humanity's tendency to fling itself impatiently into a void of annihilation. But now, I spend my time thinking about our ability to compose music and write literature, to formulate equations to explain the universe, to create engines that power crafts to explore outer space. And we're only getting started. All that we've achieved in this short amount of time is only a small fraction of our potential. The universe itself is a constant work in progress, and so are we."

He paused to take a drink.

"Our destiny," he resumed, "is a sacred place beyond good and evil. Beyond darkness and light. Beyond love and grief. Beyond violence and bliss. Beyond grace and prayer and meditation. The truth of all truths, ladies and gentlemen, brothers and sis-ters, is that we were created to return to our creators in a place of eternal creation. With that, I'm signing off. I have work to do. Beware the black-cat bones."

Alicia needed to pee. Switching to FM radio, she got up and went to the bathroom door—which was still closed, but unlocked. She opened it and stepped into the bathroom.

Her mother lay dead in the bathtub. Her blanket lay on the floor next to the tub. She had not run any bathwater, but she was naked. Her legs—shredded—were missing several chunks of flesh.

Evidently, her mother had not been killing any squirrels.

Needlessly, Alicia checked to see if her mother still breathed: she did not. She also checked to see if there was a pulse: there was not. Her mother was definitely dead.

"Thank you, black-cat bones," Alicia whispered. "Thank you for saving me from eating my own mother."

Alicia peed, washed her hands, and brushed her teeth. Then she left the bathroom and closed the door.

In the bedroom, she realized that she didn't want to spend the night in the cabin with her mother's corpse. Because it was summertime, she decided to go sleep in their car on the side of the road. It had only broken down perhaps a mile or so away. Then she could walk to the nearest town in the morning.

I'll just leave my stuff behind, she thought. *I don't need it, anyway.*

All she grabbed were an ink pen and the notebook she had been writing in recently. Clipping the pen to her shirt, she took the notebook into the living room and shoved it into the briefcase full of cash. She picked the briefcase up with her left hand and the pistol with her right.

Then she left the cabin and stepped down off the front porch.

Nocturnal insects serenaded the forest. Otherwise, the night was calm. The sky was starry, but not too dark. A sickle moon provided sufficient illumination.

Alicia took off walking down the road, but not in the direction of her mother's car. Instead, she headed toward the flashing red light of the tower behind the cabin in the distance.

Soon, she found an access road that branched off from the dirt road and led up into the hills. To Alicia, the tower's flashing red light resembled an otherworldly eye watching the trees and the ground below.

Alicia walked quickly, happy to be getting closer to the flashing red light.

After a short time, she saw a stand of trees on a ridge. Nearing the trees, she saw a small house squatting among them. The house looked very old. The tower loomed directly behind the house.

Quickening her pace, she approached the front door and leaned against it. Listening, she heard Darnell's voice. It was faint, but most certainly *his.*

Alicia tried the door. It wasn't locked. When she opened it, golden light spilled out into the night. Darnell's voice got louder. Alicia stepped inside.

Yellow bulbs hanging from the ceiling lit the small entry room. The light cast shadows on stacks of boxes and manuscripts. Darnell's voice came from a back room, somewhere behind a black curtain. Alicia walked to the curtain and pushed it back.

Darnell sat at a desk with a microphone on it, wearing headphones. He also still wore his Army field coat, with its hood over his head, and with gloves on his hands despite the studio's heat. His walking stick leaned against the desk. All throughout the room, books, folders, journals, and notebooks lay among the radio equipment.

When Darnell saw Alicia, he smiled. Then he spoke into his microphone: "To be continued. Beware the black-cat bones."

He pushed a button and took his headphones off. "Hello, Alicia! They told me that someone special was coming along to help me work, but I had no idea it was gonna be you."

"Who told you that?"

"Those who tell me that the transcendence is near, and that our preparations have become more crucial than ever. You'll meet them soon enough."

He then pointed to an empty chair next to the one he sat on. "Be seated. We have much to discuss."

PART FOUR: I HAVE NO IDEA

A MEMOIR

CHAPTER 1

I HAVE NO IDEA: A Memoir

HELLO. I'M BRIAN BOWYER, author of the three stories preceding this nonfiction piece. I'm writing this in Ohio. I'm from West Virginia, originally, but I have lived throughout the United States, and I currently live in a small city called Marion.

Now, you may be asking yourself, "Why the fuck does he live in *Marion?*" And that's a good question. Like I said, I have lived throughout the United States, but, many years ago, after attending Watkins Film School in Nashville, I moved back to West Virginia and bought a house there.

And after a while, it just got too crazy at my house. I'm talking sheer insanity—stuff I'm not gonna write about, here. I have an autobiography available if you'd like to read about any of that absolute lunacy, but I'm not trying to sell you a book. As of this writing, I am fifty-one years old, and I have plenty of money in savings.

Anyway, one of my ex-girlfriends—and I have plenty of those, too, by the way, and I still get along with all of them—contacted me. And she is a recovering heroin addict. And she had left my house about a year before, because she couldn't deal with the insanity, and she ended up leaving the state of West Virginia. And I told her that I was thinking about leaving the state of West Virginia; about just moving to a place where no one knew me, someplace I could just write and work in complete anonymity.

She said, "Why don't you come here, to Marion, Ohio?"

I said, "Where the fuck is Marion, Ohio?"

She said, "It's about an hour away from Columbus." Then she told me that her parents had moved there from Columbus, and that she had gone there after leaving the state of West Virginia.

And I said, "Okay."

So, that's what I did. I sold the house to my brother, who owns the restaurant next door, because when he found out I was leaving, he said, "Dude, if you're leaving, I want the house, because I don't want anyone else living that close to my restaurant."

So, he just wrote me a check for the exact amount that I had paid for the house, and then I put that money on top of the money that I already had in savings, and I came here, to Ohio.

And I like it.

And although I have money in savings, I also work, of course, so that I never have to *touch* any of the money that I have in savings, and I've been working at an automotive factory for the past several years.

We make brakes for Honda, but I don't work on any of the assembly lines. I am always either by myself or with one other person in one of the three drive-shaft cells: either the MDX, RDX, or the TLX cell.

And I love it. When I'm by myself, I can just work on whatever book I'm currently working on, in my head. I mentioned that autobiography earlier, but—as you probably know—I also write horror fiction and crime fiction, so I'm basically writing a horror story or a crime story at all times.

Anyway, the other night at work (I wore a toboggan), a lady stopped me in the cafeteria, and said, "Do you always wear a fucking hat?"

I said, "Not always, but frequently, because I am usually cold."

She said, "Why are you always cold? You got low blood, or something?"

Removing my toboggan, I said, "Lady, I'm six-five, I weigh 145, and I have no hair. Wearing a hat helps keep me warm."

She said, "Why don't you eat a fucking cheeseburger?"

Taken aback, I said, "Because I like Italian food, and Chinese food, and ice cream. Ice cream is my favorite."

She said, "What the fuck is wrong with you? You're always cold, and your favorite food is ice cream?"

I said, "But I love ice cream. I just wear long-sleeve shirts, and hats, and hoods. It's all good."

The lady rolled her eyes and walked away.

Then another lady told me, "Some people are so fucking rude."

I just thought the whole thing was funny.

Anyway, later that night, I was working in the MDX cell, with a guy named Ian. And a lot of the times, when I'm working with another person, I'll just glance over at them and randomly start spitting the lyrics of whatever song pops into my head—which is usually either old-school metal or hip-hop. And the other person is usually way younger than me, and they usually have no idea what I'm talking about.

But Ian's my age. He's old, like me. Well, almost. Ian's a year younger than me. Ian is 50, and I am 51.

And at some point, a Notorious B.I.G. song popped into my head, so I just glanced over at Ian, out of the blue, and said:

"Armed and dangerous / ain't too many can bang with us / we just sitting here tryin' to win / tryin' not to sin / high off weed and lots of gin / so much smoke need oxygen / steadily countin' them Benjamins, homey / you'd shit too / if you knew / what this game would do to you / been in this shit since '92 / look at all the bullshit I've been through / so-called beef with you-know-who / fucked a few female stars or two / shit, you tell me / who's the killer? / me or you?"

And Ian said, "Dude, what are you *talkin'* about?"

I said, "You don't listen to Biggie Smalls, man?"

He said, *"Who?"*

I said, "Man, never mind."

But then, sometime later, I thought, *Let's try something different.* So I glanced over at Ian again, and said:

"Lashing out the action / returning the reaction / we are ripped and torn away / Hypnotizing power / crushing all that cower . . ."

Then I pointed to Ian. "Finish it."

He said, "Dude, what is that?"

I said:

"Smashing through the boundaries / lunacy has found me / cannot stop the . . ."

I paused, giving him a chance to finish it, but he didn't.

I resumed:

"Pounding out aggression / turns into obsession / cannot kill the . . ."

I paused again, then resumed:

"Cannot kill the family / battery is found in me."

Ian said, "Dude, is that Metallica?"

I laughed. "Yeah, man. *Battery,* the first song on *Master of Muppets,* 1986."

Ian said, "Man, I *thought* that sounded like Metallica. Are they still making music?"

"Yeah, dude. They dropped an album not *too* long ago called *72 Seasons.*"

"Is it any good?"

"Yeah, man, it's pretty good. The first single was called *Lux Eterna.*"

Ian said, *"Lux Eterna?"*

"Yeah, dude. It's Latin for *eternal light.* And it sounds vintage. I'm talkin' it straight-up sounds like something that could've been on their debut album from 1983, *Kill Em All.*"

Ian said, "Hell yeah, man. I'll have to remember to look that up."

I said, "Dude, don't even worry about it. I'll send you a link."

And, of course, I went home and forgot all about it. But, the next morning, when I woke up, I remembered. I thought, *Man, I still need to send Ian 'Lux Eterna.'* So, I went to YouTube, copied the link, and sent it to him on Facebook Messenger.

Then Ian messaged me back soon thereafter, talkin' about: *Dude, you were right! That is killer! That sounds just like the old stuff!*

So, then I got in my car that afternoon to drive to work (I work 2nd shift—three p.m. to midnight), and I grabbed *Kill Em All* from one of the CD sleeves on the back seat, put it in the CD player, and listened to the first three songs on the way to work: "Hit the Lights," "The Four Horsemen," and "Motorbreath."

And, oh my god, that shit sounded so fucking good—in the car, man—real loud. I had not listened to that album in a while. The production on *Kill Em All* is so raw that it sounds like Metallica is right there in the room with you, which is part of that album's charm.

Anyway, I got to work, and I found out that I was working with Ian again, in the MDX cell. And I said, "Dude, have you ever noticed that James Hetfield lists the Four Horsemen of the Apocalypse incorrectly in the lyrics of Metallica's song *The Four Horsemen?*"

Ian shook his head. "Nope, I sure haven't."

I said, "Yeah, man. In the song, the lyrics go: *Time* / has taken its toll on you / the lines that crack your face / *Famine* / your body it has worn through / withered in every place / *Pestilence* / for what you have endured / and what you have put others through / *Death* / deliverance for you for sure / now there's nothing you can do.'

"So, in the lyrics, Hetfield lists the Four Horsemen of the Apocalypse as *Time*, Famine, Pestilence, and Death. But, in the Bible, it's *War*, Famine, Pestilence, and Death. Well, technically, in the Bible, it's *Conquest*, Famine, Pestilence, and Death. But in the Bible, conquest, in that context, means war. But out here, conquest can mean other things. But war just means war. So, when I'm referring to the Four Horsemen of the Apocalypse, I always just say, '*War*, Famine, Pestilence, and Death.'

"So, Hetfield got three of the four right with Famine, Pestilence, and Death, but Time and War have completely different meanings, so he got that part wrong. But it's still an awesome song."

And Ian said, "So, you know a lot about the Bible?"

"Oh, hell yeah, dude. I was raised in a strict, fundamentalist Christian household, and I fucking hated it. Which is why, after I became a teenage drug dealer, with a lot of money, and a fake ID, I was usually living in hotels, because I could only take my parents in small doses."

Ian said, "So, do you ever think about Armageddon, and the Apocalypse, and the Antichrist?"

I shook my head. "Not really. But I did, once upon a time, when I was eleven years old, in 1984, for a brief period of time, think that *Prince* was the Antichrist."

Ian said, *"Prince? The singer?"*

I said, "Yeah, man. You were alive back then. You know how it was. We *all* thought the world was going to end. I mean, we were all just *waiting* for it. It was almost like a subconscious *thing*, or something. We didn't know *when* the world would end, but we all thought that, by the year 2000, at the latest, all of this would be gone. I mean we legitimately believed that 1999, at the latest, would be our last year on planet Earth. Prince even wrote a song about it *called* 1999. '*They say two thousand zero zero / party's over oops / out of time / So tonight I'm gonna party like it's 1999.*'"

And back then, a lot of people spent a lot of time trying to figure out who the Antichrist was. And one of the things they would look for was a person with six letters in each of their three names, for 666.

A lot of people thought President Reagan was the Antichrist for that very reason, because his name was Ronald Wilson Reagan. Ronald: R-o-n-a-l-d; six letters. Wilson: W-i-l-s-o-n; six letters. And Reagan: R-e-a-g-a-n; six letters.

But I didn't buy it. The Bible said that the Antichrist would be charismatic, and that a lot of people would love him, and follow him anywhere. And I thought, 'Man, ain't nobody following Ronald Wilson Reagan's one-hun-dred-eighty-eight-million-year-old, crusty ass anywhere.' I couldn't even believe he got elected president. I mean, I was eleven years old and thought I knew everything. But that's what you do when you're eleven, right? You think you know everything.

But Prince was *very* charismatic, and a lot of people loved him, and a lot of people would have followed him anywhere.

And he also had the whole six-let-ters-in-each-of-his-three-names-thing going for him with Prince Rogers Nelson. Prince: P-r-i-n-c-e; six letters. Rogers: R-o-g-e-r-s; six letters. Nelson: N-e-l-s-o-n; six letters.

And I also knew that, according to the Bible, Lucifer was one of the most beautiful angels in Heaven, before he got cast out, and that he was a master of music.

Back then, a lot of people used to say that the media itself was just the devil. Back then, in the 1980s, a lot of people used to say that the media was just Satan controlling the airwaves with his music.

And Prince certainly controlled the airwaves with *his* music, in 1984, when he dropped not only the movie, *Purple Rain*, but the soundtrack. And there's a song on that soundtrack called "Darling Nikki," and it's one of the songs that made Al Gore's wife, Tipper Gore, form the PMRC, the Parents' Music Re-source Center, which was the organization that was respon-sible for putting all those explicit-warning, parental-advisory stickers on the albums—which only made the kids wanna listen to the music even more, so the whole thing was stupid.

And back then, a lot of us had whatever albums we liked on both cassette *and* vinyl. We had the cassettes for our boom boxes, and our Walkmans, or whatever. And we had the vinyl albums so that we could read the lyric sheets, and the liner notes, and look at all the photos, or whatever. So I had both, the cassette *and* the vinyl album of the *Purple Rain* soundtrack.

And there was a backward message . . . there *is* a backward message . . . at the end of the song, "Darling Nikki." Now, if you only heard the song in the movie, you wouldn't know that. But if you had the soundtrack at home, like I did, and listened to it, you heard it. And a lot of people may have heard that and just thought it was Prince speaking gibberish, but I knew immediately that it was a backward message. Dude, this was 1984. This was the height of the entire Satanic Panic thing, and we fucking loved that shit, man. I mean, if we even heard a *rumor* that an artist or a band had a backward message in one of their songs, we got excited and came running.

So, that's what I did. I went to my younger brother, and I said, "Dude, there's a backward message on this *Purple Rain* soundtrack."

And he said, "Fuck yeah!"

So, we put the album on the record player, put the turntable in neutral, dropped the needle on the vinyl, and began spinning the album in reverse, so that we could listen to the backward message.

And lo and behold, Prince said, "Hello. How are you? I am fine. For I know that the Lord is coming soon. Coming, coming soon. Ha, ha, ha, ha, ha, ha, ha."

And I said, "Dude, Prince is the fucking Antichrist. He just told us all that he is happy that the rapture will be happening soon, and that God will come down here and call all of the Christians home to be with him, and Jesus, and all the angels in Heaven, allowing Prince to rise as the Antichrist and rule planet Earth."

And my brother said, "Dude, you're fucking right, man. Prince is the goddamn Antichrist."

And we. Fucking. LOVED it! We fucking loved Prince, man. I still do. I miss that motherfucker.

Now, of course, I didn't believe that for very long. Maybe a week or so later, I thought, *Man, that's some stupid shit. Prince ain't the fucking Antichrist.*

But yeah, for a brief moment in time, in 1984, when I was eleven years old, I thought Prince was the Antichrist.

Just a silly story that I shared with a guy at work, and I thought I would share it with you.

But check this out: a few nights later, I was working by myself, in the RDX cell, and I got tagged on TikTok by a book reviewer, by Ricky at Ricky's Rockin' Reviews. He had just finished reading one of my horror novels that I mentioned earlier.

He said, "Brian Bowyer: I have noticed that a lot of your characters spend a lot of time in basements, and I'm wondering about the significance of basements in your fiction. And I'm also wondering if *you*, Brian Bowyer, have spent a lot of time in basements. And, if so, would you tell us one of your basement stories?"

I said, "Man, that's a good question. I've never even thought about that. *Basements.* Yeah, Ricky, I got a *lot* of basement stories . . ."

My first memory of a basement is being raped in one at age four.

Is *that* the significance of basements in my fiction? I have no idea. And I'm sure there are many people in twenty-first century America, and all throughout the world in all prior centuries, with far worse stories of sexual abuse than mine, but that *is* my first memory of a basement: being raped in one at age four.

And it happened a *few* times, actually.

What happened was, my mother's father—my grandfather, Bill—died before I was born, so I never knew him, then my grandmother remarried when I was four. She married a man named Leland, and he had two mentally-challenged teenage children: an eighteen-year-old daughter named Jean, and a sixteen-year-old son named Lee.

And Jean was slightly *more* mentally challenged than Lee, but Lee was significantly mentally challenged. He was also morbidly obese, so he was way bigger than me. Plus, he was sixteen, and I was four.

And they all moved into my grandmother's house, the grandmother to whom my mother was very close. So my mother would take my younger brother and me over there, frequently, so that she could visit her mother. And Lee would take me down into the basement and rape me.

Why didn't I tell anyone? Because I knew, at age four, that it would hurt my mother more than it hurt me.

But I did get sick of it. So one day I grabbed a butcher's knife from my grandmother's kitchen, and I took it with me down into the basement and brandished it. And I told Lee that if he ever touched me again, I would fucking kill him. And he believed me. And he never touched me again.

And that was that.

Okay, fast-forward two years. I'm six years old now, and my younger brother is four. I was in first grade, but he hadn't even started kindergarten yet. And one night, he attacked me in my sleep. We had been sharing a bedroom on the first floor at my parents' house.

Our parents had a nice, finished basement, but my brother and I almost never went down there. Our mom did laundry down there, in the basement. And she and our father often watched TV in this huge family room down there, in the basement. But my brother and I shared a bedroom on the first floor.

And one night, while I was dead asleep, he started screaming, "Give me back my fucking milk!"

I opened my eyes, and my younger brother was standing over me.

I said, "What the fuck are you talking about?"

Then he started punching me in the face, still screaming, "Give me back my fucking milk!"

I yelled, "Mom! Dad! Come and get this motherfucker!"

So they took him to a hospital. And it was discovered that he had what is called *encephalitis*. I had never even heard of it. It's an inflammation of the brain that makes your brain swell inside your skull, and it causes hallucinations.

And he started having recurring *bouts* of encephalitis throughout the next few years of his childhood. And it kills some people. And it gives some people permanent brain damage. But he was fine. It just went away after a few years and stopped afflicting him, and now he's this genius who has owned his own restaurant for the past twenty-eight years.

But that's not *all* he does. I mean, my brother is *super*-smart. I could write whole volumes of books about my crazy-intelligent brother. But yeah, he has owned Mickey's Pizza in Beckley, West Virginia, since 1997. He took over that restaurant when he was 22.

Anyway, fast-forward another year. I'm seven years old now, and my younger brother is five. I was in second grade, and he was a kindergartner. And one day, we got off the school bus, and our house had burned to the fucking ground. Our parents were at work, and we had been at school.

At seven years of age, I *was* my younger brother's babysitter. At seven years of age, I was basically a young adult.

Anyway, the driveway was long, and it was filled with firetrucks and cop cars, and the house was completely fucking gone.

The house had been heated by a modern furnace, but our mom and dad also had this old-fashioned, wood-burning/coal-burning stove, down in the basement, in that family room, and the fire inspectors determined that the stove was what caused the fire.

Our parents had insurance, so they built another house on the property, but we had to stay elsewhere while it was being built.

After it was finished, as we were moving in, my parents asked me if I wanted my own bedroom.

I said, "Fuck yeah," because A) I wanted to get away from my psycho younger brother, and B) Who doesn't want their own bedroom?

So they gave me a room downstairs in the basement.

And the basement was only partially submerged in the earth, because the house was built split-level into a hillside, but the room they gave me was in a corner of the basement that was *completely* submerged in the earth. So there were no windows, and when I turned the lights off, it would be pitch black, and I fucking loved it. I loved sleeping that way. Plus, you could tape posters floor to the ceiling, all the way around, without any windows getting in your way, so I always had a lot of heavy-metal posters on all the walls, floor to ceiling.

And there were drop tiles *for* a ceiling, so you could hide drugs, and money, and guns and stuff up there, which was fucking awesome. But that was later, because when I first moved down there into the basement I was only seven years old. But later, after I became a drug dealer at age twelve, that drop-tiled ceiling *definitely* came in handy.

Anyway, I started drinking when I was eleven, and I was an alcoholic by age twelve, and I became a drug dealer, at age twelve, to finance my addiction. I had several older cousins who were members of the Avengers Motorcycle Club, and they were all drug dealers, and they sold me drugs for cheap, and I turned around and sold cocaine in the 1980s for crazy profits, so I always had a lot of money.

And a lot of the time, I'd be living in hotels, with fake IDs. But, when I wasn't living in hotels, I'd be staying at my parents' house, in the basement.

And there were two entrances into the basement, one on either side of the house, where it was built split-level into that hillside on the back. And I had keys to both doors, so I could come and go as I pleased, at any time, day or night.

At age twelve, my parents could not control me. And they knew that. They didn't even try. So, when I was there, I always had a lot of older friends coming in and out of the basement.

And older customers coming in and out of the basement.

And older girls coming in and out of the basement.

Sometimes there would be girls going out one door of the basement while other girls came in through the other door.

And of all the countless, insane stories I could tell you about that basement, I'm going to tell you one that is memorable to me because of the viciousness with which a mother punched her daughter in the face, down there in my old bedroom in that basement.

I had been out the night before with a girl named Alice and her friend Stephanie. I was fourteen at the time, too young to drive, so I had one of my older friends driving us around.

Years later, Alice's friend Stephanie ended up getting her fuckin' head blown off with a shotgun, by a member of the Avengers Motorcycle Club, for cheating on him. But on the night I'm writing about, I'm pretty sure that Stephanie—like me—was fourteen.

Anyway, Alice had to be home that night, at midnight, so I had my friend drop Alice off at her mom's house.

Then Stephanie immediately turned to me and said, *"I* don't have to be home tonight. Can I just stay with you?"

I said, "Yeah, sure."

So, we went back to whatever house party we had been at, and then I took Stephanie to my parents' basement around dawn.

And we passed out . . . a little later.

And then the doorbell rang, upstairs. But we never heard that, of course, because we were passed out.

And my parents weren't home, but my younger brother was home, and he heard the doorbell. So he got up and opened the door.

And it was Stephanie's mom and Alice, standing on the front porch.

After Stephanie had not come home the night before, her mom had gone to Alice and said, "Where the fuck is Stephanie? She was with you last night, and she never came home."

Alice said, "I don't know. Last time I saw her, she was with Brian, and I just thought Brian was going to take her home."

And my brother had no idea that Stephanie was there, because his room was upstairs on the first floor, and we were downstairs in the basement. So he let them in the house, and they came downstairs and started pounding on my bedroom door.

And there was music playing, because I always slept with music on.

And Stephanie said, "Oh my god, Brian, that's my mom. She's fucking crazy. You don't understand."

I said, "Whatever, man. Just go hide in the closet," because I had this huge walk-in closet.

So then I got up and opened the bedroom door.

And Stephanie's mom said, "Where's Stephanie?"

But I never even had a chance to answer. She shoved me out of the way, started looking around the room, opened that closet door, found Stephanie, and then she punched her so hard in the face, she knocked her the fuck *out.* Then she grabbed her by the hair and dragged her out of the bedroom.

I turned to Alice, and I said, "God*damn.* Was that *necessary?"*

But Alice was pissed off. She said, "I can't *believe* you fucked Stephanie." Then she turned around and stormed out of the room.

Anyway, I hope that gave Ricky at Ricky's Rockin' Reviews some insight into the significance of basements in my fiction.

And then, a few nights later, I was working in the TLX cell, with a new guy—way younger than me; maybe half my age, if that. And he had just gotten out of prison. And he had heard that I had been in prison.

I said, "Nah, dude. I retired from crime when I turned eighteen. Before that, however, I was in and out of juvenile prisons."

He said, "What were you in juvenile prison for?"

I said, "All kinds of stuff. I was a teenage drug dealer, but I was also involved in *other* criminal activities. And, because I was young, brash, and reckless, I spent a *lot* of the 1980s incarcerated in juvenile correctional facilities."

He said, "Dude, tell me one of your juvenile prison stories."

I said, "Man, I got a lot of those. Well, let's see here. I could tell you one about a girl named Tish. You wanna hear one about a girl named Tish?"

He said, "Hell yeah, man! Let's hear it."

I said, "Okay. I first met Tish in 1989, when I was sixteen, in a juvenile prison called the Salem Industrial Home for Youth, in Salem, West Virginia—which is also where I began reading horror fiction at age sixteen. There was a correctional officer there named Moscar, an Italian dude who happened to be a huge horror fan, and he started bringing me books every day by anyone who had published anything in the genre at that time, which was 1989: Stephen King, Dean Koontz, Clive Barker, Robert McCammon, Richard Laymon, Jack Ketchum, the list goes on and on . . ."

Girls, also, were incarcerated in Salem.

Picture Salem as a sprawling college campus, with a lot of large brick buildings, all of it surrounded by twelve feet of chain-link fencing, with three feet of razor wire on top of that. It was maximum security.

The girls were locked up in a building with two halls called *Standard* One and Standard Two, and the boys were locked up in a building with two halls called *Jones* One and Jones Two, but the boys and girls commingled quite a bit.

We didn't go to the cafeteria together, but we did go to the school building together, and we often found ourselves in the gymnasium together, and the library building, and the computer lab. Yes, there was a computer lab, in 1989. Primitive, but it was there. And we often found ourselves outside together, if the weather was nice. And *if* the correctional officers liked you, they facilitated *alone time* for the boys and the girls who were dating, so it wasn't too bad.

The first girl I started dating was in there for murder. I don't remember what her real name was, but everyone called her VO5, because some of the other girls caught her masturbating with an Alberto VO5 shampoo bottle, before I even got there. She was older than me, almost eighteen, and I had just turned sixteen, so we didn't date long, then VO5 turned eighteen, and got sent to the women's penitentiary, to begin serving the rest of her life sentence.

The second girl I started dating *also* happened to be in there for murder. She was my age, sixteen, about a month older than me. She was this sweet, shy, really pretty girl named Tish, and she didn't even seem like she belonged there.

Then I found out that Tish had never killed anyone. She had simply been with her boyfriend—a much older boyfriend—when he killed someone, and they charged her as an adult.

They offered Tish a reduced sentence if she would testify against him, but she refused, and they threw the book at her, gave her life without parole.

Oh, and that boyfriend, for whom she threw her life away? He never contacted her again. I just thought the whole thing was sad.

Anyway, eight months passed, and my time was up. It was time for me to go home. I was still sixteen.

"Are you gonna call me?" Tish said. "Are you gonna write to me? Are you gonna come and see me?"

"Yes, yes, and yes, baby," I said.

But I never called her. I never wrote her a letter. I did not go see her.

But I wasn't out long. I got arrested soon thereafter, and then I got locked up in Salem once again.

And of course Tish was still there—as she would be, until she turned eighteen, when she would be sent to the women's penitentiary, to begin serving the rest of her life sentence.

"You're back!" Tish said, when I returned. "I've missed you so much, baby."

"I missed you, too."

"I hope you're not mad," she said, "but I was so happy when I heard you were coming back."

And of course I wasn't mad. Tish and I picked up right where we had left off, and I resumed reading horror fiction for the next eight months.

And then, once again, my time was up. It was time for me to go home. I was seventeen, now.

"Are you gonna call me this time?" Tish said. "Are you gonna write to me? Are you gonna come and see me?"

"Yes, yes, and yes, baby," I said.

But I never called her. I never wrote her a letter. I did not go see her.

I went right back to my fast-lane lifestyle, and Salem was three hours away from my hometown of Beckley, West Virginia.

Anyway, I was seventeen, but I didn't live with my parents. I was selling drugs again, and living in hotels on Harper Road.

One day, however, for whatever reason, I stopped by my parents' house on a weekday. My parents were at work, my younger brother was still in school, and the telephone rang.

This was 1990. We didn't have caller ID in 1990. In 1990, if the telephone rang, to find out who was calling, you had to answer the phone and say hello.

So that's what I did.

And it was Tish, calling from Salem. "Brian! I miss you so much!"

"I miss you, too."

"Why haven't you called me?"

"I'm sorry, Tish."

"Why haven't you come to see me?"

The truth was, I had not been planning to go see her.

I don't know if you've ever been incarcerated before, but when you're locked up, you make a lot of friends, but then you get out and you never see those people again. Or at least, that's been my experience, anyway.

But then she told me that she was having trouble sleeping—that she would be turning eighteen in a couple of months, and that she was terrified of being sent to the women's penitentiary to begin serving the rest of her life sentence.

"I wish I had some sleeping pills," she said. "I just wish I could sleep."

And then, just like that, I knew that I *would* be going to see her. I hated the thought of Tish not being able to sleep, and I had the ability to get her any kind of sleeping pills she wanted.

"I'll be there Saturday," I told her. "What kind of pills do you need?"

"The only ones that really work for me," she said, "are Seconal and Nembutal. Think you can get me some of those?"

"I'm sure I can," I said. "Just hang tight. I'll be there Saturday."

"Thank you so much, Brian. You'll never know how much this means to me."

I had never heard of Seconal or Nembutal, but I got off the phone with Tish, called my cousin Dominick at the Avenger's clubhouse, and he told me that I could pick up a bottle of each the following day.

Then I ran into my friend Tracy, later that night, and I said, "Dude, you wanna go to Salem this weekend? I'll pay for all the drugs, alcohol, cigarettes, gasoline—you name it."

He said, "Fuck yeah! Road trip!"

So I picked the drugs up at the Avengers clubhouse the next day, then Tracy and I traveled three hours to Salem on Saturday.

We listened to Slayer, drank whiskey, and did cocaine the entire trip. By the time we got there, we were wasted. Tracy went into the cafeteria with me for the visitation. There was a guard nearby. I don't remember his name, but of course we knew each other, and we had always gotten along. He was reading a paperback novel and didn't pay any attention to us at all.

And Tish was acting *so weird*. I mean flat-out bizarre is the best way I can describe it. I had never seen her like that. I figured it probably *had* to be the insomnia, but it made me a little uncomfortable nevertheless. Apparently it made Tracy uncomfortable too, because he said, "Look, dude, I'm gonna head on back to the car and drink some more whiskey. Take your time."

I was actually relieved when the guard looked up from his book and said, "Five more minutes. Need to wrap this up."

I had a lubricated, tied-off condom in my pocket. In the condom was a 100-count Tylenol bottle. In the bottle were fifty Seconals, fifty Nembutals, and enough cotton to ensure that the pills wouldn't rattle. I took the pills out of my pocket, then leaned in close to Tish and used my back to shield her from the guard while she slipped the bottle down her pants and up inside herself.

"Thank you so much," she whispered. "You'll never know how much this means to me."

And that was that. Tracy and I left and headed back to Beckley.

Then I got locked up in Salem *again*, less than two months later, for the dumbest reason.

Here's what happened:

I was walking the streets of East Beckley one night with my friend, Cousin It. His real name was Ronnie Smith, but people called him Cousin It because of his hair and his resemblance to a character on a TV show. He's been dead for years, but at the time he was twenty and I was seventeen. It was very late, probably three o'clock in the morning, and we had just left The Nuthouse, for some reason.

The Nuthouse was just a nickname for a building called Tanner Apartments that my friend Billy Young's grandmother owned. It was three stories tall, but it also had an attic and a full basement. There was one kitchen and one bathroom on each of the three floors that were shared by all the people who rented the five bedrooms on each level, and the place was always packed with junkies, drug dealers, alcoholics, prostitutes—you name it.

At seventeen, I had been using The Nuthouse as a sort of criminal headquarters for years. It was right across the street from the State Police Headquarters, on Eisenhower Drive—so they would be watching us with binoculars, and we would be watching them with binoculars, and cops raided the place all the time.

But they never found my ever-changing stockpile of stolen guns up in the attic. They never even went up *into* the attic, actually, which could only be accessed through a trapdoor in the ceiling of Billy's closet on the third floor.

Anyway, I don't remember why Ronnie Smith and I left The Nuthouse at three o'clock in the morning, but I *do* remember what we were arguing about as we walked those otherwise empty residential streets. Like me, Cousin It was a huge Clive Barker fan, and we had been arguing over which of his novels was the best. Ronnie's favorite was *Weaveworld.* Mine was *The Great and Secret Show.*

Then a car stopped right beside us on the street, and a man behind the steering wheel put his window down and said, "Is there a problem?"

For no reason.

I saw a gun next to him on the passenger's seat. I had no idea why he stopped and asked us that, but I pulled *my* gun—a Taurus PT92 9mm—from the waistband of my jeans, shoved it into his face, and said, "Not unless you want one, motherfucker."

He stepped on the gas and drove away. And that was that. We didn't think anything else about it.

The next thing I knew, it was daylight, and Ronnie and I were annihilated. We were back at The Nuthouse, in the kitchen on the third floor, drinking whiskey with two other dudes at eight o'clock in the morning.

At some point, we all realized that we were hungry. I volunteered to go to the Super America gas station down the street and get us some food. They all gave me some money, told me what they wanted, and I took off walking.

Super America was only about a minute or two away. *It* was right across the street from the State Police Headquarters, so I didn't think anything of all the cop cars in the parking lot. There were always cop cars in the parking lot. That was nothing new. I had no idea they were looking for me. I was fucked up, but I wasn't staggering, or anything. I had a gun in my waistband, but I always carried a gun. I wore baggy clothes. They couldn't see my gun. I wasn't worried about those cops.

I walked into the store, got everyone's food, and then as soon as I stepped outside, the cops surrounded me.

"FREEZE, BOWYER! HANDS IN THE GODDAMN AIR!"

They took my gun, handcuffed me, and placed me under arrest.

I said, "What the fuck am I being arrested for?"

They told me that the man who had stopped his car earlier and asked us if there was a problem—for no reason whatsoever—was an off-duty police officer. I did not know that man, but he knew *exactly* who I was. He had gone straight to the police station and pressed charges against me after I shoved my gun into his face.

I said, "Man, I should have shot that motherfucker." That's what I told the arresting officer. Then I said, "Fine, man. Take me to Salem. I'll hang out with Tish and read horror fiction. I'll be eighteen in a couple of months, then I'm retiring from all this crime bullshit anyway."

My first day back at Salem, Moscar stepped into my cell, laughing. "You just can't stay away from this place, can you?" He was holding a thick hardback book.

"Is that for me?"

"Yes. Stephen King. *Four Past Midnight*. Have you read it yet?"

"No, I haven't."

He handed me the book. "It's his latest release. I just finished it, so it's all yours. You're gonna love it."

"Thanks!" I said, eager to read the latest from Stephen King.

Moscar turned to leave, but then he turned back around. "Oh, I just wanted to tell you how sorry I am about Tish. I know you two were close."

I looked up from the book. "What are you talking about?"

Moscar cocked his head. "You haven't heard? Tish is dead, man."

"Dead?"

"Yes. I assumed you would have heard."

"Nah, dude. What happened?"

"Suicide, I guess," he said. "Unless she just accidentally swallowed enough barbiturates to sedate a fucking squadron. No idea how she got *those* in here, Brian."

"Dude! I didn't know! I swear to God it never crossed my mind. She told me she couldn't sleep."

"I'm sure she *couldn't* sleep, Brian. The prospect of spending the rest of your life in prison, at eighteen years of age, would make anyone have trouble falling asleep."

"You do believe me, though, right? That I didn't know?"

"I *do* believe you, Brian. And if I were Tish, I would have done the same thing. And if I were you, I would have done the same thing even if I *had* known what Tish was going to do. Don't beat yourself up about it. Enjoy the book."

I did my time and they turned me loose when I turned eighteen. And that was the day I officially retired from a life of crime.

And that is *another* reason I love my job at the factory—because I get to tell stories to other people; which is all I really like to do, anyway: either read stories or write stories.

And, speaking of stories—thank you very much for reading these.

I hope you have an amazing day or night.

About Brian Bowyer

Splatterpunk Award-nominated and Godless Award-winning author Brian Bowyer has been writing stories and music for most of his life. He has lived throughout the United States. He has worked as a janitor, a banker, a bartender, a bouncer, and a bomb maker for a coal-testing laboratory.
He currently lives and writes in Ohio. You can contact him at brian.bowyer@hotmail.com.